My Family Business

When There is No Choice

Nick-Anthony Zamucen

Dedication

Throughout my life, I have feared no man. I have learned that fact is indeed stranger than fiction, and people are generally good. If one learns to compete with only oneself, the outside world becomes just a distant vision. Learn to keep distractions at bay and always focus on what's most important in life… family.

Gavin, Cali, and London, all I do, all I am, and all that is good is with you.

(PS)

About the Author

Nick-Anthony Zamucen is an award-winning serial entrepreneur. This is his fourth book but first fiction book. His other books include: Flip It, Maverick Franchise, and Bits of Wisdom. All three titles are non-fiction, but this book dives a bit more into Nick's creative side.

With three beautiful children and an adoring wife, Nick's time is the most valuable commodity. Writing is his takeaway from working. As Nick continues to create multi-million dollar companies, he will always have a creative outlet that needs to be nurtured.

Life is always happening for us, not to us.

Preface

"I never wanted to be a gangster..."

My Family Business is the fourth book by Nick-Anthony Zamucen. This being Nick-Anthony's first fiction book, we follow the character of Nico, as he struggles to keep his morals while being forced to help run the family business.

Born to a family of mobsters, the death of his brother flings Nico into a rabbit hole of secrets, long hidden by his family. This exciting story, packed with backstabbing, love, family commitments, and gunfire, stops readers from putting the book down at any stage.

Read as Nico wrestles with accepting his fate to become a gangster and clutching onto his morals. Will he succumb and run the family business?

Grab your copy of 'My Family Business' now and find out.

Contents

Page Left Blank Intentionally

Chapter 1
As a Boy

I never wanted to be a gangster. I mean, if you think about it, no child born in a typical household with sober parents, a good education, and food on his table would want to be a gangster. It doesn't make any sense why a child would wish to follow in such footsteps.

If I go back to the beginning of my memory, it was my 15th birthday. I remember waking up with the sun shadowing my closed eyes. Annoyingly, I arched my arm over my eyes and stretched restlessly on my platform bed. I was comfortable for the first few minutes, but the light seemed to creep its way from under my arm. So, I gave up and finally woke, rubbing my eyes.

I searched the room for my clothes that lay crumpled on the floor outside of the bathroom, next to my broken baseball bat that I thought I would get fixed. But I never came around to get the job done. An old alarm clock with a broken ear sitting on the dresser next to my trophies struck 8:00 a.m. I searched for my slippers, but they weren't there. I sighed to myself and called out for Chloe.

Usually playful in the morning, our family dog – a small terrier with stringy grayish hair – loved playing with any slippers found unattended. She often pulled them under the bed and made a pillow out of them. When she didn't respond, she usually waited for me to come and get them from her. She and I would then enjoy a game of tug of war, followed by wet kisses and back rubs.

From the outside of the room, I heard Mama's voice, calling out for me. I quickly jumped back into the bed and pretended to sleep.

"Nico, are you up?" Asked Mama from the doorway.

"I am now," I said, rubbing my eyes and sitting up straight.

"Happy Birthday, Il mio bambin! How did my little boy sleep?" Mama said as she walked toward me and leaned in to give me a big hug and a kiss.

"Mama, I'm not a kid anymore," I said as I erased the lipstick stains from my cheek and tried to free myself from her arms.

"Alright. How did my big boy sleep?"

I made a face at that, to which she said, *"Don't make faces at your mother. You're just 15. You'll always be my kid. Now get up and get dressed. Papa's waiting for you downstairs, and I'm making breakfast."*

After this, she left the room. I jumped out of bed and stood in front of the mirror, taking a good hard look at myself. I was in good shape for a 15-year-old. I was five-foot-five and weighed almost 115 pounds. Five more pounds, and I'll be perfect for the school's football team.

After taking a shower, I dressed and made my way downstairs to the kitchen where Papa, Carlo, and Valeri were already seated around the table, while Mama served everyone pancakes. Carlo was seven years older than me, and Valeri had just started kindergarten. Everyone wished me birthday.

First, Papa hugged me, patted on my back, and called me a young man. He was a gentleman. He never yelled at his children nor hit them. If you were looking for genuine advice and wanted someone to hear you out, he had always been there. He went through a lot in life. When he was just 15, his family had migrated from Italy to the United States. On his way to the States, he lost his parents. He then raised himself on the streets of Brooklyn, where drugs, alcohol, and crime spread like Black Death. He worked as a small town hustler and numbers runner until he met Mama in his 20s. He fell in love with her and moved to San Francisco for a fresh start. On the other hand, Mama belonged to a better part of town. Her parents were a part of the administration. They expected their daughter to follow in their footsteps. However, her destiny was tied to Papa's fate. Her family disliked him.

To convince them to like him and think that he was a good match for their daughter, he started driving a local bus. Eventually, the business prospered, and today, he is the owner of a tourism bus-line service that runs nationally from coast to coast. The business made us rich. I remember there were times when Papa had to stay away from home for weeks because he loved his job, Mama, and us.

However, there was something about him that I never really understood. He was always secretive. He didn't talk much and was always reading the paper. Sometimes, he would get a phone call in the middle of the night and leave without informing anyone. After he broke his leg in an accident, he always worked from the basement of our house. Neither we, kids, nor even Mama, was allowed to enter the basement without his permission.

"So what's the plan for today, Nico?" Papa asked sternly.

"Nothing much, Papa. I'll just lay around the house and maybe go visit Luca," I said.

Papa nodded at that and went back to eat his breakfast. Carlo was second to wish me with a pat on my shoulder that sent a sharp pain down my spine. He really wasn't the nicest brother one could wish for. Since he was the oldest, he was better in almost everything. He was a bright student at the school. He did great at sports and also had his way of charming the ladies, while I struggled to get Sophia's attention who lived just across the road.

Papa and Carlo would work hours in the basement, and never let anyone else in. Papa always said that I would follow them in the family business, just like Carlo, but I was not sure about it. I wanted to get a college degree first, become a lawyer, and move to another city with Sophia.

"I think your Mama has some plans for tonight," said Papa.

"Really, Mama?" I asked in surprise.

"Yes, Il mio bambin. Call Luca and your other friends. Carlo and Papa are inviting their guests as well. And I've asked the neighbor kids to come over too," she said.

"The neighbor kids?" I asked, hoping she invited Sophia too.

"Yes, lover boy. Mama invited Sophia too if that's what you're asking," interrupted Carlo with a grin.

"Shut your face, Carlo," I said back.

"Shh...both of you. Carlo, go buy groceries if you're done with breakfast. The list is on the counter. Don't forget the butter. And Il mio bambin, you want to help me?" She asked.

"No Mama, I'm going to my room to read," I said as I left the kitchen.

As I came back to my room, I looked outside the window, hoping to catch a glimpse of Sophia across the street. I saw the lights in her room go out. That proved she knew I was secretly watching her. I had a crush on her since we moved into this house. She lived across the street, opposite my house.

She and I went to the same school but took different classes. Luca, my best friend that I met in History class, was the only one who knew how strong my feelings were for her. There were occasions when I tried expressing my feelings to her but failed miserably. Sophia had long blonde hair, blue eyes, and rosy skin. Sometimes, when I think of her, I feel a warm tingly feeling. It was a weird feeling, but I knew how to handle them – cold showers.

The football team coach always said, *"Cold showers, boys."* So cold shower it was.

I spent most of that afternoon reading, *'Gone with the Wind,'* and fell asleep while reading. Not only did I enjoy reading but also on a Sunday afternoon, when the sun was too bright, and there was not much to do, I fell into a deep slumber. I woke with a start. I usually don't dream, but I woke up sweating from a terrifying dream. I saw my family. I saw Mama, Valerie, and I, but I could not see Papa and Carlo. Mama looked sad and old. We lived in a two-room apartment. It was dirty and lacked all the basic necessities.

At night, we sat around the table, waiting for Papa and Carlo to come home. We were poor and did not have food to eat, let alone afford education for Valeri and me. The bell rang, and I opened the door. There was Papa covered in blood, sweat, and tears. But the blood was not his. He held Carlo in his arms. Carlo's lifeless body was staring at me. And a dog with severe blows to its eyes, one ear cut off was standing next to Papa, with blood dripping from its wounds too.

It was my dog. It was Chloe. She was dying. I was too numb to move. I heard a woman scream, Mama most probably, and then woke up, gasping for air.

"Nico, you okay?" Asked Carlo as he stood in the doorway.

I jumped out of bed and ran forward to hug Carlo. No matter how much I pretended to dislike him, I couldn't bear the thought of losing him. After all, he was the one who first taught me how to shave. He helped me solve math problems when I couldn't. And he stood up for me when I was bullied in school for having big ears.

"Woah! Easy there...are you okay?" He asked again.

"I love you, Carlo. Please don't leave me, please," I begged, holding him tight.

He pushed me away from him and said, *"Relax weirdo, I just came to tell you that the guests will be here soon. Mom wants you to dress up and come down."*

Carlo left the room, but I stood there for a while, trying to contemplate what had just happened. I searched my wardrobe, looking for something reasonable to wear. Since Sophia was coming too, I had to make sure that I looked my best. After 20 minutes of trying out different outfits, I finally decided to go with a gray-colored shirt and black plaid pants that grandma and grandpa had sent over for Christmas. I combed my hair back and made sure they were all in place.

Just then, I heard Mama call my name from downstairs, *"Nico, Luca is here. Come down."*

I quickly ran down to greet Luca.

"Hey man, what's up? Happy Birthday," said Luca, giving me our usual fist-bump and half hug.

"Hey, thanks! Dude, the game is on. Let's go watch," I said as I led him to the living room.

It had been only 15 minutes when Luca and I started watching the football game when the guests began to arrive. But my eyes only waited for Sophie. I had to put Chloe back in her room, as crowds made her really nervous.

I went back downstairs into the living room. My Uncle, Mike, and Papa were standing with a few of their friends. They called me to them. Papa and all the other men were smoking cigars in the corner of the living room. I walked over to them and held out my arm for each one of them.

"Happy Birthday, Nico," they all greeted me.

"Thank you, Uncle Mike. Thank you, sir," I smiled at all of them.

"It seems like only yesterday he started going to school, and look at him now, a young man already, ready to take part in his father's business," said Uncle Mike.

Papa smoked a puff on his cigar and nodded in agreement.

"He's a big boy with brains. Soon, he'll be able to give you and Carlo a hand in the business. I'm sure Nico's already excited to start working with his Papa, right boy?" Said Mr. Ray, who was Papa's childhood friend from Brooklyn's old days and a business partner.

Following Papa and Carlo in the business was not what I wanted. My instinct was to contradict with their thought, but then decided to stay quiet. It wasn't the right time to bring it up. As the men continued to talk about business and politics, I politely excused myself to the kids' area that mom had arranged.

I was surprised to see that Sophia was already there, and I had not noticed. With Luca by my side, I tried to gather some courage to talk to her. While we still argued about how I would go up to her and talk, I felt a soft hand on my shoulder. Terrified to the core, I turned around to find Sophia standing with a perfectly wrapped present in a golden wrapping paper that resembled the shade of her hair.

"Happy Birthday, Nico," she said, holding her hand out.

Too stunned to reply, I stood there simply staring at her, looking like the most beautiful thing my eyes had ever laid eyes on. Luca gave me a slight push, which helped me come back to reality.

I quickly took her hand and said, *"Thank you."*

"This is a really nice party, Nico. Please tell your mom I said, Thank you for inviting me."

"Sure, sure, I will," I replied hesitating.

Right when I was starting to gain some confidence around Sophia, Mama interrupted our small rendezvous.

"All right, everyone, gather around the table. We're going to cut the cake," she said excitingly and to me, *"Birthday boy, the cake is waiting!"*

I have to be honest that I was a little embarrassed by how Mama treated me. Papa and his friends thought I was old enough to take part in the business, and here, Mama thought of me like I was still a five-year-old.

Mama loved baking and often did it as a hobby. But when times were challenging, she started baking part-time for the neighborhood to make some extra money on the side. Of course, Papa could not know about this. So, she managed to keep it a secret from him all these years. But after Valerie was born, she decided to stop baking and become a full-time mother. Also, Papa's business was going so well, and we were doing a lot better financially.

Everyone gathered around the table. Luca stood at my right arm while Mama and Sophia stood at my left. All the guests sang me the birthday song. I was happy to see all my family and friends together in one room. There was nothing more I could have asked for.

The cake-cutting was followed by snacks, a dance, and some party games. Thanks to this party, I was able to talk to Sophia! Apparently, Luca was confident around girls, and his confidence had helped me become friends with her. Surprisingly, we happened to have the same favorite books, which also gave me a chance to talk about something without hesitating. The best part was that I was lucky enough to get Sophia's phone number, and we soon decided to go to the library together.

Luca's parents were out of town, so he was going to have a sleepover at my house. After the party, we were too tired to do anything. Luca and I just lay in my room and recalled the good moments. He then took out a box of cigarettes from his pocket and started lighting one.

"Woah man, when did you start smoking?" I asked.

"Doesn't matter. You should try it too. They're such a relief, Nico."

"No way, and keep that box inside, I don't want my parents seeing you with cigarettes. They'll think you're a bad influence," I explained with exasperation.

"But I am a bad influence, and you know that, right?" He said with a smirk.

"Yes, but if they find out, they'll stop me from hanging out with you. My parents are strictly against drugs and such stuff, man," I protested.

"Alright, alright, relax Mr. Goody-Two-Shoes."

"I am going to get some water. You want something?" I asked him.

"Nah, I'm good."

I entered the kitchen and poured myself some water. It was nighttime, so I wasn't expecting anybody in the house to be up, which was why I was surprised at first when I heard screaming from the top floor. I followed the voices. The noise was coming from my parents' room. Papa had got drunk at the party, but that could not be the reason. He got drunk quite often. I knew it was wrong, but I could not help overhearing. Mama and Papa never fought. I ambled really close to the door, putting one ear on the wood. The voice, my Mama's, sounded quite angry.

"Yes, I know about it. How long did you think you could hide it from your family? Why Marco, why put our lives at stake? I thought you stopped this when we got married," Mama yelled at Papa.

"How do you think I provided for all of you, huh? Where do you think all this money was coming from? The bus service? No, Marie, it was the manila envelopes that you always asked about. Look, I get my money from kickbacks. My drivers drop the tourists to these restaurants in North Beach that pay me commissions from their profits. I built the North Beach, Marie. It is because of me that place is doing so well. It is the place where you love eating out, don't you?

It was money from these deals that paid for all the lavish expenses. God, you're an ungrateful woman, Marie."

Commission? Deals? For a second, I thought I was dreaming again. I pinched myself to feel something. Turned out I was not dreaming. And what I was feeling now was a rush of emotions and mixed feelings that were too hard to explain.

"You're a liar, Marco. I can't believe you betrayed your own family. Oh, my God! You involved Carlo in it, too. How could you, bastard?"

"Look, Marie, I'm just trying to secure our kids' future. They will be happy. We'll never be short of money."

That was the voice and tone Papa used to placate Mama.

"We don't want your money. I can't trust you, Marco. I just can't. You have to choose; it's either us your family or your secret business."

There was a long pause, and nobody said a word.

"You can't make me choose! I run this house. You don't give me orders, woman. I'm telling you, Marie, stay out of it. It has nothing to do with you. Dammit! It's just a simple transaction from the restaurants that I get. Don't make such

a big deal out of it. And this conversation is done. We're not talking about this again. You understand me?"

"I don't know what else to say," she said.

"Go to bed Marie. It's late."

I could not believe what I just heard. My parents, who I thought were the epitome of love, the people I always looked up to, were fighting like this. They're not perfect. They lie, they betray, and they do wrong. What was harder to digest was that all that time, my Papa kept us in the dark. He lied to Mama. He lied to us. Carlo knew that too. And then, Papa wanted me to join him in this filthy business as well.

I did not know what was going to happen next. What decision Mama was going to make. I had just turned 15. Was I supposed to think like an adult or a teenager? I quietly went back to my room. Luca was asleep, and his cigarette box was on top of the side table. My whole life until that point seemed like a lie. Nothing made sense at that moment. It felt like my mind was going to explode.

I remembered what Luca said, *"It's a relief."*

At first, I hesitated. This is not what my parents would like, but then they are not perfect either. That night was one of revelation and unveiling of lies and secrets. It was also the night when I smoked my first joint.

Chapter 2
Death before Eyes

I stood impatiently on the corner of Market St. and Haight St., behind the school waiting for Luca. The clock in a shop across the street showed a quarter past two. I'd give him a few more minutes, then I'd leave for home without him. The pain of my father's shocking revelations was still afresh in my mind.

The news of Papa's secret business and Mama hiding it for years had kept me wondering for two nights in a row. What other secrets have they been keeping from us? It was surprising how they went about by the day like nothing ever happened. Little did they know that I had heard everything and was now a part of their dirty little secret.

A black Ford Bronco pulled up to the curb in front of me and honked loudly. I looked at it.

"Hey Nico, come over here," Peter Givenchy and Russell Crew, known for their bad reputation in school and the neighborhood, were calling me.

I slowly walked toward them. What did they want from me?

Russell opened the back door. *"Hop in,"* he invited. *"We'll drive yuh home."*

"Thank you. But why would you drop me home?" I asked with a confused look.

"Good question. Let's just say we're in a mood of helping, and it's your lucky day today," said Russell with a smirk on his face.

"But…" I thought about Luca, and how he would react if he found that I accepted a ride from the guys who bullied him in junior high.

Peter and Russell were tall, muscular guys with a thick South American accent. They ate children's lunch in junior high, and as we all grew and entered the sophomore year, the intensity of their bullying and pranks increased considerably. They now mocked boys and girls for their appearances, the way they talked, how they dressed, and how timid they were.

There was one incident when both the boys tricked an exchange student, robbed him of his money and lunch, and dropped him at a deserted place with no food, water, or even a cell phone to call anyone. The student later, with the help of a few locals, was able to make his way to the school's dorms. Russell and Peter were both suspended for a month but came back with new tricks and ideas to torture the other kids in the school.

"Hurry up, Nico, we haven't gotten all day, boy," shouted Peter from the front seat.

Russell pushed me in the back seat before I could protest. I guess Luca would have to walk home alone. I sat quietly in the backseat, trying not to make a sound, but the toxic smell of cigarettes and the deafening metal music made it hard for me to sit still.

"So yuh into Sophia, huh?" Shouted Peter over the loud music. *"She's fine, whatcha think, Russell?"*

I instantly started regretting this ride.

"Tell us, Nico, how yuh scored with Sophia. Teach us some moves, man," said Russell.

"She's just a friend. We barely talk," I justified, hoping they'd let go of the Sophia topic.

"My house was just around the corner, you missed it," I said panicking.

"Who said we were taking yuh home?" Said Peter. *"Yuh comin' with us, Nico."*

It was at this moment when I realized that I had made a stupid mistake by accepting the ride.

"Peter, I have to be home by 3. Drop me home," I pleaded.

"Why? Your momma waiting for yuh, dressed up?" Said Russell chuckling under his breath.

"Shut up and let me go."

"Sit down, Nico," shouted Peter. *"We're not gonna kidnap you. We just want yuh to play with us. So relax."*

"Play with you?" I asked.

"Ahan! You got that right," said Peter pulling his car a few meters away from a basketball court.

"Yea, we had a game with the boys, and we saw yuh standing at the corner of Market St. doing nothing, so we figured yuh could help us win."

Considering my past two days had been just me locked up in my room smoking the cigarettes I stole from Luca's bag, a basketball game sounded refreshing. It could help me clear my mind at least.

"Nico! Hurry up," shouted Russell.

I ran to catch up with them. The boys already at the court were throwing the basketball back and forth to each other. They stopped when they saw us coming. I could see five dark, muscular boys, three feet taller than me. They were of the same age as Russell and Peter. I was the only odd one out and didn't belong there.

"Who's the kid with yuh?" Asked one of the guys in khaki pants and a white vest. He seemed like he was the dominant one among all the others. He had broad shoulders, a sharp haircut, and a two-inch deep cut on his right arm.

"He's on our team, Xavier. You gotta problem?" Said Russell.

I tried not to look offended when all the other boys saw me and laughed. They thought I was small and weak. To be honest, I was offended and wanted to look good for them now, more than ever. As we proceeded with the game, the ball came toward me, over my head, but I jumped and took a stab at it.

The ball caught the top of the rim and rolled in. That made the seventh point I scored out of the 13 for my team. The ball came back into action. I missed what seemed like a few easy shots, but each time they were improved. When the ball seemed to be going to the other team's guys, I stole a quick glance at a gun that was lying on the bench next to Xavier's belongings.

From behind me, I could hear Peter's sudden shout, *"Nico, Your ball."*

I turned around quickly. Russell threw the ball floating freely toward me. I set myself ready to catch the ball. Xavier, on the other side of the court, flashed up before me, took the ball from me, and hit the ball on the ground hard that it came back bouncing at me.

As a reaction, my hands went up to cover my face, but I wasn't fast enough, and the ball hit me square in the face, which caused me to tumble to the ground. I got up on my feet angrily, one side of my face red and cut where the ball had hit me. Xavier, on the other side of the court, was grinning at the sight.

"That was a foul," I yelled at him.

He was no longer smiling.

"What's the matter, Nico?" He scoffed. *"Yuh think you're the only athlete in the game?"*

I made my way for him, but Russell's hand gripped my shoulder firmly and stopped me. I took my position back on my side of the court. The ball again shot directly over my head, and Xavier jumped for it. I beat him to it and swatted it hard right back at him. The ball struck him squarely in the face, and he fell on the concrete floor. I mocked loudly at him. Xavier got up from the floor, darted toward me, and tackled me around the legs.

We rolled over and over, punching and clawing at each other. His voice was harsh and angry in my ears when we were tousling, *"You little ginny!"* Russell, Peter, and the other boys tried to pull us apart, but we started at each other again, roughhousing. He was stronger than me and more powerful. He held me down from both arms. I tried to hold him away by raising my arm – the way I had seen fighters do in the movies.

The other boys had now stepped back and were enjoying the fight. A flash exploded in my eyes. I could hear the boys begin to cheer. Another flash exploded. I felt a sharp cutting pain in my ear, and then on my mouth. There was a weird buzzing sound in my head.

"This is a mistake. This is a mistake," I kept repeating in my head.

I shook my head anxiously, clearing the voice, and opened my eyes to look. Xavier was standing in front of me, laughing. The blow had hit me when I wasn't looking. I got up on my feet, anger running throughout my body. My throat was raw, and I could feel my breath stinging against it. I held my arms up, trying to call it quits, but he came in charging for me with another blow. I ducked and smiled to myself. It made sense now. I just had to try to keep my head on my shoulders.

Feeling a bit confident, I waited for him to come to me again. As he came toward me, I drove my hand right into his stomach. His knees began to buckle, and I took a step back to gain my balance and reengage. I used this opportunity to hit him twice in the face. He straightened up, and his face was red with anger now.

As he made his way back at me, I could feel a rush of adrenaline through my body and into my arms. I bent a little and brought my right arm up from the ground. It caught him right under the chin. I could feel what seemed like an electric shock throughout my body.

Xavier spun around and fell flat on his face on the ground. I stepped back and looked at Russell and Peter. Their faces were flushed, staring down at Xavier on the floor. Peter's tongue was running nervously on his lips, and his fists were clenched. There was a sudden silence on the court. I looked around at the other boys, and their faces were flushed too.

"Run Nico, RUN," shouted Russell.

Peter and Russell started to run. Russell grabbed me from the back of my shirt and pulled me to run with them. We sat in the truck and quickly drove away from the court and out into the streets.

I turned to look from the back seat. The boys were surrounding Xavier in a circle.

"Nico," Russell pulled me back on the seat from behind and said, *"We'll drop yuh off to your home, and yuh stay there, got it?"*

I nodded silently, not sure what I was supposed to say. As much as I loved this feeling, I was scared to death and could not clear the picture of the gun from my mind. It definitely belonged to Xavier.

"Look, Nico, if you love yur life, then lay low. We better not see yuh on that side of the town anytime soon," Peter

said, as he stopped the car a few feet away from my house.

"Today was fun, but yuh betta watch out for Xavier." He said, *"Now jump out, we'll see ya later. Lay low man."*

I watched them take off, as I stood on the corner of the lane with sweaty palms and blood dripping from the edge of my mouth. Xavier's blows had left me with a black eye and a fat lip. I didn't know how I was going to explain it to Mama.

***

The clock in the hallway struck 5 p.m. I was supposed to be home two hours ago. I tried to make my way silently to my room without making a sound and hoping nobody noticed my absence.

"Nico, is it you?" Shouted Mama from the kitchen.

I did not respond.

"Luca called and said you did not walk home with him today," she continued.

I silently kept moving toward the stairs when a tight grip on my shoulder stopped me from moving forward.

"Answer your mother, young man," came a groveled voice from behind.

I turned around to see Papa standing behind me.

"Yes, Papa," I replied while facing him.

"What happened to your face, Nico?" Papa questioned.

Before I could answer, Mama walked into the hallway. She looked tired. She had just finished cooking and cleaning the entire house.

"What happened to my baby?" She screamed in bewilderment as she looked at me.

"Who did this to you? Tell me Il mio bambin, what happened?"

"Calm down Marie, I'm asking him," said Papa, as he pushed her aside, who had already started to tear up.

"Answer Nico, why you are late, and who did this?" He asked.

I hesitated first, not sure if I should tell him the truth.

"I...I...I was at a game."

"What game?" He yelled louder than before.

"Um...Market St. I...was playing basketball with some friends from school, and I...I fell and I...I lost track of time."

I was shaking and could not look Papa in the eyes.

"You sure you're not lying to me, Nico?" He raised his voice.

"No...no Papa, I'm not lying to you."

What was happening to me? This wasn't me. I don't steal, I don't smoke cigarettes, I don't accept rides from the bad guys, I don't punch guys with guns, and I definitely don't lie to Papa.

I could feel tears welling up in my ears. I clenched my fists and tried not to show my emotions. I just wanted to go to my room.

"Nico, look at me," he said.

After a moment's hesitation, I looked up at him and then Mama. She was watching me with sadness in her eyes. She was afraid what had happened to Papa might happen to me too.

Papa's face was calm and more relaxed now. He had believed my story.

"Go to your room Nico, and clean up. And then come back downstairs in 20 minutes. Your Mama will set you up something to eat."

"Yes, Papa."

I made my way upstairs to my room without looking behind. I heard Mama sob, but I turned a deaf ear to her cries. It was unusually quiet in the house when I realized that Papa had sent Carlo to San Jose on a business trip. Valerie had gone for a play date at the Smiths, and it was just Mama, Papa, and me in this big house. I thanked God for not having Carlo around. He always knew when I was lying. I'm not sure how he did that, but he could figure I was lying by just looking at my face.

Before stepping into the shower, I quickly peeked outside the window, hoping to catch a glance of Sophia. Her curtains were drawn, and the lights were off. She had still not returned from visiting her grandparents in Brooklyn. I missed seeing her reading at her desk, studying late nights, or brushing her hair, and that one time when she stepped out of the shower, with wet hair and her… *"Ouch!"*

I stepped back in panic, as Chloe leaped out for me from under the bed, where she was hiding and waiting for me.

"Easy...easy, big girl," I told her, as she licked my face and pushed me to play with her.

"Missed me, huh? I missed you too, baby girl. Long day."

I rubbed her back and tossed her a biscuit that I had kept hidden from her for quite some time. I quickly took off my sweats and ran a cold shower. The water was freezing, but my bruises still burned. I dressed up, combed my hair, and ran downstairs. Papa was in the living room watching the local news, and Mama was sitting on the dining table, waiting for me to come down.

"Il mio bambin, come here." She said, *"Show me your bruise."*

"Mama, I'm fine," I pushed myself away from her.

"Shh..." She pulled me closer to her and applied some ointment that she had already prepared.

"Ouch, it hurts," I complained.

"Shh... Stand still, Il mio bambin."

She applied a Band-Aid and was happy with the work she had done on me.

"Now sit down and eat, I made meatball soup."

As I sat to eat my meal, Papa came over and joined me too. He sat on my left and waited to be served. Mama went to the kitchen to grab another bowl and some bread for him.

"How are you feeling now?" He asked.

"Much better, Papa."

"Good."

Mama entered the room and started serving him the soup.

"Nico, Uncle Mike will be here in an hour to pick you up, so finish your schoolwork before that," said Papa.

"Where is he taking me, Papa?" I asked in confusion.

"Your Uncle and I have decided that since you'll be joining your brother and me in the business soon, it's better for you to start learning now."

"But Marco..." Mama turned from the doorway and made her way back to the room. *"He's too young."*

"Stop it, Marie, we're not having that conversation again. It's decided that Nico will be joining us in the business, and he starts today."

His face was stern.

"But Papa..." I hesitated. *"I don't know anything about the business."*

I lied again.

"Don't worry Nico, Uncle Mike will show you the ropes."

"But Papa... I..."

"No more buts Nico. You're going."

We finished the rest of the meal in silence. An hour later, the doorbell rang. I was sitting in the dining room, completing my schoolwork when Papa and Uncle Mike entered.

"Hey Nico, Nico!" Uncle Mike patted on my back.

He was tall and had the same mustache as Papa's, except he was always in a good mood and made everyone laugh at his jokes.

"Hello, Uncle Mike."

I took his hand. His grip was firm, and his palms were sweaty.

"So, ready for your first lesson, big boy?"

He seemed more excited than ever. I silently looked at Papa and then Uncle Mike. Their eyes were bright with excitement. Papa stood there, with hands in his pockets, standing tall, as his second son was about to follow in his footsteps. Little did he know that I wanted to run away, far and far away from this hell hole he was dragging me into.

"Oh, he's more than ready, Mike," Papa answered on my behalf.

"Well, we better get going, before it gets any late, gotta bring Nico safe home too huh," he said jokingly.

As we drove in Uncle Mike's black SUV, it was already dark. The sky was a shade of dark blue, and the birds were flying higher than usual.

"Where are we going, Uncle Mike," I asked.

"We're going to tie up some loose ends, Nico."

"What kind of loose ends?"

"You ask a lot of questions, you know?" He said, half questioningly.

"Look Nico, the business your father and I are in can be risky. There are a lot of bad guys, some good guys too, but mostly bad guys. You know your father runs a bus service, right?"

"Yes, I know."

"That is just a side business. The buses run up to North Beach. We drop the tourists there and receive hefty kickbacks from all the restaurants and clubs. Your father basically runs North Beach, big guy."

"But, isn't that wrong, Uncle Mike?" I felt my voice rising.

"Calm down, Nico. There's nothing wrong with it." He said as the car came to a stop next to an old gas station.

"Now listen, I'm going to go in the store, get something and come back in a few minutes. Till then, I don't want you to move or get out of the car. You get me?"

I silently nodded, watched him get out of the car, and walk toward the store. There weren't a lot of cars or people around; just one black, rugged truck parked in the rear end of the shop. It probably belonged to the store owner, I guessed.

The view of the store from the car was clear. I watched Uncle enter the store and shake hands with the man standing behind the counter. They smiled and talked for a few minutes. Uncle picked up a few cigarette packets from the shelf and went back to the counter. The man bent down and recovered a yellow envelope from under the counter.

There were so many of these envelopes in our basement, where Papa worked. It was the same one. He handed the envelope to Uncle Mike when a few guys walked from the back of the store to the front where they were standing. I recognized them immediately. It was Xavier and the gang. I started sweating and panicking in the car. I did not want him to see me, so I slid down in my seat. The car was standing at a distance, so it was impossible for them to notice me, but I could clearly see everything. What I saw next sent chills down my spine. Uncle Mike was talking to Xavier. He was alone, and they were five. At first, it seemed like they knew each other, but slowly, it started to turn into a heated argument. I could not figure out what was going on and watched silently from a distance.

Xavier was a dangerous guy and owned a gun. I could not tell if he was Uncle Mike's friend or an enemy. But I knew that something was not right, and I was helpless. The argument continued for a few minutes when one of Xavier's boys punched Uncle Mike in the face. The man behind the counter appeared to be very calm as if he wanted this to happen. The next thing I know, Uncle Mike had a gun in his hand and was pointing it in Xavier's face.

"Put the gun down, Uncle Mike. Please put it down," I repeated in my head.

The man from the counter yelled something at Uncle Mike. Right then Xavier cowardly tried to throw a sucker punch in Uncle Mike's face but missed wildly. It was at that moment when I heard a loud gunshot. Someone was shot. It was Xavier. Uncle Mike had shot Xavier in the head and watched as his body crumbled to the ground in the store. He stood over Xavier's dead body and stared at him for a few minutes, pointed to the shop owner, and said a few words and calmly walked out. I was sweating, my eyes had become watery, and I was unable to see clearly. Panic flowing throughout my body.

What do I do? Is getting out of the car a good idea? Was this part of the deal? Or something had gone wrong?

There was a loud knock on the car window, and there was Uncle Mike with Xavier's blood on his shirt, telling me to unlock the door.

I quickly opened the door with shaking hands.

"We gotta go, Nico," he whispered under his breath.

He started the car and turned for Lombard St. at full speed.

"What happened, Uncle Mike? Who were those guys?"

He did not answer.

"What happened, Uncle Mike?" I repeated.

"Why did you shoot the man?" I yelled.

The car came to a sudden stop, and Uncle Mike looked me in the eyes.

"Look, Nico, this is normal. It happens in business sometimes. Remember I told you, there are lots of bad guys. Well, these were the bad guys, Nico. So calm down."

He seemed relaxed as if he had done this many times before.

"I'll drop you home now, and you go to bed, it's late. And of course, don't ever talk about this, you understand? This is our family secret Nico, you're going to be a huge part of it. Don't ever rat out, ever. Trying to be a hero gets you hurt in this business. Nothing comes before family, don't forget that. Now let's get you home, your mother Marie, she is a bit of a worrier."

If this was my family's secret, then I did not want to be a part of this family, I thought to myself.

We drove in silence, and he dropped me at home by 8:30 p.m.

"Good night Nico, and remember, nothing comes before family, nothing." He said.

I simply nodded, too numb to respond. The front door was open. I made my way inside and was going toward my room when I heard Mama call me from the lounge.

"Il mio bambin," she called.

Mama was wearing a white gown and sitting in the lounge, reading a copy of Agatha Christie's *Death on the Nile.* The lights in the room were dim. Her face looked older than she really was. I had forgotten how beautiful she looked in this white gown. The wrinkles on her face were deeper than ever, and the sides of her mouth curled in a smile when she saw me enter the room.

"Yes, Mama," I said as I sat next to her on the sofa.

"You look so pale, Nico." She touched my face.

"What happened, my child? Tell me, please."

My skin grew colder, and my eyes filled with tears. I looked up at her and broke in a cry.

"What's wrong, Nico? Tell me," she insisted.

"Uncle Mike... He... He shot someone at the store, Mama." I dug my head deeper in her lap.

"My baby," I heard her mutter under her breath.

"I'm sorry, Nico. I'm sorry you had to see that, baby."

I could feel her warm tears on the back of my neck. She was crying too.

"Nico, Look at me now. You will not become like your father nor your Uncle. I will make sure that doesn't happen," she held me tight from arms.

"You will not be in this business Nico, and I promise to keep you safe baby, I promise."

She pulled me in and hugged me tightly. Now that the cat had been let out of the bag, I went upstairs to my room and threw myself on the mattress. Chloe was fast asleep under the bed.

Was I really supposed to become like my father? How do I say no to him? What about Carlo? Has he killed someone too? I punched the same man, Uncle Mike shot. What were they talking about in the store? Did a deal go wrong? Did Xavier know I was related to Uncle Mike? What was he doing there?

These were the questions I didn't know the answers to. I decided to light a cigarette and surrender myself to whatever lay ahead of me.

Chapter 3 – Part A
Loss of a Brother

"Nico! Il Mio bambin, come down," called out Mama from downstairs. *"Breakfast is ready!"*

I heard her call out for me loud and clear, but I decided to ignore it just like I ignored the warm sun rays hitting my face. I twisted my body and adjusted in the bed, my back now facing the curtain-less window. Not sure how long I had been sleeping, I pulled the comforter over my head, hoping to catch five more minutes of sleep before Mama came upstairs to wake me up.

It was Saturday, no school that day. Luca and I had planned to go to Lake Merced for some fishing and fun. He was a member of the school fishing team and often went on national tours. He had even won prizes. I had convinced him to teach me how to fish, as I badly needed a hobby to distract myself from the recent experiences at my home.

I turned around, squinted, and reached the alarm clock resting on my side table when a hyper Chloe jumped from underneath the bed to me.

"Chloe!" I cried in panic, as the alarm clock slipped from my hand and hit a glass of juice beside it, spilling juice all over the wool carpet.

"Girl, look what you did," I scolded her while she looked at me with soft blue, puppy dog eyes and made whimpering sounds.

I quickly grabbed an old T-shirt from the closet and started scrubbing the carpet. It didn't work. It merely made the stain worse on both the carpet and my T-shirt. Chloe was a friendly dog. I had rescued her from a garage sale where Papa had taken Carlo and me. She was a small dog with brown with gray patches all over her body. Her previous owner had abandoned her, and I found her hungry and covered in fleas. She was scared, hiding behind a car, and making loud whimpering sounds.

I had traced her cries to the far end of the garage. She had leaped at me just like she did today. It took Papa some begging, but he could see how happy Carlo and I were by finding Chloe, so he agreed for us to take her home. Since that day, Chloe and I become the best friends. She lived in my room, and I took her on walks every day. Chloe continued looking at me with her soft blue eyes that I could not resist. I threw the cloth away, and we both strangled in a friendly fight, which usually ended up with me on the ground and her on top of me, licking my face, and giving me wet kisses.

"Is that what you've been doing for so long?"

Carlo was standing in the doorway with his arms folded across his chest. He looked different since the last time I saw him before leaving for the trip. My big brother was all grown-up and looked much older than he was. The sunlight in my room highlighted his broad muscles and the stubble on his face. His voice was manlier, and he looked taller than usual.

"When did you come back?" I asked.

"Last night, when you were sleeping." He said casually, *"What happened to your face?"*

"I fell playing basketball," I said, hoping he would not catch my lie.

"You sure, you got that from playing? That's a disgusting bruise, man!"

"Yeah," I whispered and nodded my head.

By the look on his face, I didn't think he was going to believe my story. He stood there with his arms crossed and a questioning look on his face.

"Anyway, didn't you hear Mama calling you? Wash your face, and come down. We're waiting over breakfast. Papa's here too."

Carlo left the room with Chloe by his side. I grabbed my juice-stained T-shirt and tossed it into the laundry basket next to my desk. On my way to the bathroom, I stopped to catch a glimpse of Sophia but decided to leave it for later. My bruises were healing as I looked at myself in the mirror. However, there was a deep brown scab left on my forehead. It looked ugly. I tried to cover it with my hair but failed miserably.

The scab was prominent and reminded me of Xavier, every time I looked at it. It reminded me of him, who was now dead; shot by my Uncle. For the past two days, I was trying to push these thoughts to the back of my mind, but somehow, they always made their way back to me when I least expected. Just like all the other times, I pushed them aside, washed my face, combed my hair, and made my way downstairs where everybody was already seated around the table.

"Good morning, Papa," I said slowly but audible enough to hear.

"Good morning, Nico," he replied sternly, not looking away from the newspaper in front of his face.

"Sit down and start breakfast, Il mio bambin. We have a long day today," said Mama, as she lay a plate of blueberry pancakes in front of me.

Carlo was sitting opposite to me on the seat next to Papa, while Valerie fed Chloe most of her breakfast. We ate in silence for some time.

"After breakfast, I want both of you to go to your rooms and pack some clothes. We're going to your grandparents' house," said Papa as he kept the newspaper aside and began eating his food.

My grandparents lived in Virginia City, Nevada, which was a four-hour-long drive from San Francisco. Every year on their anniversary, we traveled to their house and celebrated till late in the night. We would often stay in the town for two more days after dinner and then come back home. This was the only time we saw our grandparents. They were very traditional yet hospitable.

They would feed us with all kinds of Italian food and make sure we went back home with full stomachs and beautiful memories.

"I was planning to go fishing with Luca, Papa," I said.

"You can go fishing some other day, Nico. It's your grandparents' anniversary. Don't you know we go every year?"

I looked down at my hands in my lap, disappointed. Uncle Mike will be there too. I had not seen him since the shooting took place at the gas station. Not sure if I was ready to see him again at all.

"We all can go fishing some other day. Your grandparents will be happy to see all of you," said Mama.

It was clear, I had no say in the plan. The decision was made. We were going to spend the weekend celebrating my grandparents' anniversary in Virginia City.

After breakfast, Papa went off in the basement, working on some of his deals. Mama had cleaned the kitchen and was packing Valerie's, Papa's, and her clothes for the weekend. Carlo and I quietly made our way to our rooms to pack our stuff. We all were supposed to meet downstairs again in half an hour.

I threw myself on the bed and stared at the walls. *Was anything ever going to go my way?* I thought to myself. I wanted to get a law degree, but it seemed like Papa had other plans for me. I wanted to go fishing, but we had to celebrate my grandparents' anniversary, in which I had no interest. *When will my parents stop treating me like a child?*

My thoughts turned from myself to Carlo. I wondered why he never protested against any of Papa's decisions. Was he willing to do everything Papa asked him to do or had he accepted it as his fate? Does Carlo have any plans for his future? Does he have a secret girlfriend? I heard him talking to a girl on the phone once, but I wasn't sure. A part of me sympathized with my older brother, but then a part of me had no idea who he really was, and what he wanted.

I realized that I had wasted 15 minutes thinking about things I had no answers to. I quickly threw in a few T-shirts in my backpack. There wasn't much that I wanted to carry with me. Just a pair of fancy shoes for the party, dress pants that grandpa had gifted me last year, my sunglasses, and a book to read on the way. I went downstairs where everyone was already dressed up and loading in the car. Mama had prepared some sandwiches and snacks for the trip. Valeri was asleep in Mama's arms and was not at all bothered by the course of actions that was gradually transforming our lives. She was so lucky, she did not have to think about life, her career, and what she was going to do in the next three years, at least not now. We all waited for Papa, as he locked the house and took control in the front seat. Trips to my grandparents' house were always awkward. No one spoke at all, except Valerie. Carlo sat in the passenger seat next to Papa, while Mama, Valerie, and I sat in the back seat.

Most of the time, I read my book, while other times, I looked outside the window at the clear blue sky and the passing scenery. After a four-hour-long drive, we finally reached Virginia City. It was a small city that was famous for the Comstock Lode. Back in the day when we used to go there, I remember we would stop at saloons, ride steam engines, and take a tour of the industrial area located between Denver and San Francisco.

After Mama and Papa had gotten married, my grandparents moved to Virginia City from Brooklyn because they wanted to stay close to their daughter. Mama visited them often in the early days of their marriage. Later, when Carlo was born, and then I came, the visits grew less, and eventually stopped, except the yearly visits on their anniversary. It was a small city where everyone knew each other. With time, the population of the town grew, and it became famous for tourism. Grandpa and Grandma lived in the quieter part of the town. They lived alone in a big house made out of red bricks and pinewood. Every time we visited, Grandpa took us to the famous candy shops for fresh fudge and ice cream cones.

We finally reached their house and were greeted by my grandparents, who embraced all of us in hugs and kisses. Mama was excited to see her parents. This was the only time in the year when I saw her genuinely happy and thrilled. Grandpa shook hands with Papa and led him into the house, probably to the bar while Carlo and I unloaded the car.

The party was at 9 p.m. My grandparents were famous in the town for throwing grand parties. They invited everybody they knew. They were liked for their generosity and hospitable nature. Mama and Grandma had already taken control in the kitchen, talking about food, drinking juice, and preparing for the event, while Grandpa and Papa sat at the bar drinking scotch and smoking cigars.

"Where is Mike? Why didn't he come with you, Marco?" Asked very excited Grandpa.

"He had to run some errands. He'll be here before the party starts," Papa answered, sipping his drink.

"Hey, kids," Grandpa yelled, as he saw Carlo and me bringing our bags into the house.

"I've set up the room for ya'll. I figure y'll would be tired of all the traveling and needing some rest, maybe."

"Woah! Thanks, Grandpa. I'm gonna have to stretch my legs," said Carlo.

"Yeah, me too. I'm exhausted," I added.

"Don't forget, boys. The party is at 9," he waved one of his hands at us while holding a drink in the other.

Since we were kids, Carlo and I shared one room at our grandparents' house. It seemed like nothing had changed. The room had our toys, a few of our clothes at the time when we were small, and some old jewelry that belonged to Mama.

"Get your shoes off the bed, Carlo."

I pushed his legs from my side of the bed and made some space for myself.

"Shut up, Nico. I'm tired," he lay there with his arms covering his eyes.

We both lay in silence for the next 10 minutes.

"Carlo?" I asked, turning my face toward him.

"Hmm...," he said half-asleep.

"Can I ask you something without getting you freaked out?" I asked.

"Depends, but go ahead."

"Are you happy working with Papa?"

My question caught him by surprise. He supported himself on one arm and lay facing me.

"What do you mean, Nico?" He had a confused look on his face.

"I mean... do you like the work and taking orders Papa gives you? And are you happy?"

"First of all, I don't know why you're asking this, Nico. Second, yes, I'm happy working with Papa. He knows what's good for his family, little brother. And I suggest you listen to him too," he sounded like he meant it.

"But don't you have any other dreams. Don't you wanna be something else than doing the family business?" I pushed.

"Honestly, no! What's better than being in your family business, Nico? Nothing, but you're too young to know that. Once you join Papa and Uncle Mike, you'll realize family is all that matters."

I wasn't sure how to react. I thought Carlo was my only hope to get out of this mess. But, it turned out that he loved working with Papa and Uncle Mike. There was nothing I could say to change his mind.

"But, Carlo... don't you think?" I started again.

"Shh... Nico, no more questions. Let me sleep."

Carlo was hard to break, but I wasn't going to give up either. I decided to try some other time. For now, I turned back to my side and dozed off.

***

It was dark when I woke up. The other side of my bed was empty, where Carlo was sleeping before. I rubbed my eyes and tried to gain consciousness. There was a faint shadow of the moonlight in the room. My eyes moved to the wall clock in front of me. It struck 9:30 p.m. I was late. Nobody woke me up. I had been sleeping for too long. I could hear the faint sound of music. The party had begun, and I was still not ready.

There was no time getting mad at Mama for not waking me up as usual, so I quickly grabbed my ironed clothes from the hanger and put them on. I had started to gain weight since my last birthday, and all my clothes were growing short on me. It took me a couple of minutes to fit into my clothes, but I managed. I took a long hard look in the mirror before leaving for downstairs. I looked quite decent and tall for my age. I guess it ran in the family.

The party was in full swing, as I went downstairs. The room was full of people I had never seen. I tried to find familiar faces from my family, as I walked ahead when I felt a hand on my shoulder, gripping it hard. I turned around to see Uncle Mike standing in a blue suit with a glass of wine in his hand.

"Nico, hey man, how are you?" He asked with a big smile on his face.

The events of the shooting night were still fresh in my mind. But I tried not to show it on my face, and instead, remain as calm as possible.

"Hello, Uncle Mike, I'm good. How are you?" I said politely.

"I'm good, Nico. It's been a while since I saw you, since... you know... that day."

We both knew what day he was referring to.

"Anyway, have you seen your father or Carlo anywhere?"

"No, not really! Papa may be at the bar with Grandpa," I said.

"Alright, young man. Have fun."

Uncle Mike's breath smelled of alcohol. He always had a low tolerance for it. Most days, when he got drunk, Papa would let him crash on our couch. Mama was strictly against it, but he was Papa's younger brother, so no one could say anything to him, not even Mama. As the party continued to flow through the night, the guests became drunker and louder.

Mama stood under the chandelier, her white gown sparkling under the golden lights. Her smile was so broad that it showed off her perfect set of white teeth. She was beautiful. I didn't notice how gracefully she was aging. One could tell she was a beauty in her time. She waved at me from across the room, and I waved her back as a sign that I was having a pretty good time, even if I wasn't.

With not much to do at all, I decided to make my way to the bar where all the men were gathered talking about politics, games, and business. As I reached the bar, I saw that Carlo was standing in the corner of the room with Papa, Uncle Mike, and a stranger on his side. They all were talking in hushed voices, difficult for me to decipher. They all had a drink in their hands except for Carlo, who looked down at the ground with sunken eyes. Since I had nothing much to do there, I made my way toward the door. As soon as I was about to leave the room, I heard Papa call out for me.

"Hey, Nico. Come here," he called.

I walked toward him and the three other men standing beside him.

"Nico, this is Consigliere Miriam Katz, my childhood friend and one of the best lawyers from coast to coast," he said proudly.

I extended my hand and greeted Mr. Katz with a polite smile. His grip was firm and warm.

"You've grown into a big boy, Nico," he laughed. *"I remember when you were just a little boy, and look at you now, all grown-up."* His laugh was loud and shook the entire room.

Not sure how to answer, I quietly nodded and smiled.

"So when are you joining your Papa and Uncle in business, big boy?" He asked.

"I... I'm not su..."

"Very soon," answered Papa before I could even finish my sentence. *"He'll join us soon, Katz."*

I excused myself and came out of the room with Chloe wagging her tail beside me. I hadn't had a chance to walk her out since we came to the city. The dining hall lit brightly with glittery dresses and perfectly polished chandlers. The women danced, laughed, and ate cake, while the kids of my age played in the corners of the room. Chloe tugged hard on my pants.

"Okay, okay, we'll go," I told her, as I tied her harness and dragged her into the night with me.

Since my grandparents lived in the east end of Virginia City, they were surrounded by thick trees and acres of barren land – a good place to harvest the crop in the summer and to simply take dogs on a walk. I tried not to go far from the house, in case I lost my way back home. The night was unusually dark and quiet. The birds were asleep, and the only sound one could hear from a mile away was the loud music and drunken locals partying. No one knew that I had left. I hadn't planned to go further than two miles, from where I could easily spot the house and return safely. Chloe and I walked deeper into the woods, played catch, and chased one another. This was way more fun than attending a party full of old men and women. The night had started to creep in when I decided to go back to the house. I heard a sound of hushed voices and stopped for a second.

I might be imagining, I thought to myself, when I heard the voices again. It sounded like people talking. Their voices echoed in the woods. What would someone be doing at this hour of the night? What if they had also been taking their dog out for a stroll? But the night was too dark, and it was hard to see. I walked further into the woods, hoping to catch a glimpse of the voices coming from behind an old oak tree.

My heart was racing, and my palms were sweating. I tried my best to remain calm. There was a sudden uneasiness about this night. Chloe was unusually quiet too. I'm glad she did not make a sound, which helped us from getting caught. I slowly peeked from behind the tree to the front, where a pale moonlight revealed two dark figures, standing tall. Their faces were blurred, and their shadows were too dark for me to see from the distance.

I tried to stay as quiet as possible, but with a dog by my side, it became difficult to stand still. Both of the men were tall and spoke in graved voices. One of them was unable to stand still and kept limping on his side. Who were these men? What were they doing in the middle of the woods near my grandparents' house at this time of the night? Were they siblings, like Carlo and me? Or did they share a bond much stronger than that?

One of them murmured something slowly. The other man nodded his head and moved two steps back to turn around when the first man pulled him closer and punched him hard in the face. He fell on the ground and made a loud cry for help. My body was shaking. I had witnessed a scene similar to this a few days before. Today, I stood frozen and numb, unable to move a limb or say a word.

The tree's bark covered my identity from revealing to the men, who were now strangling each other, rolling on the ground of thorns and wild bushes. Chloe was scared too. Unlike any other dog who would have barked and made their presence known, she stayed close by me, circling between my legs. The men were on their feet again and began talking. One voice now sounded more like pleading and begging for mercy.

The man who looked a lot younger and was probably more injured moved toward the older man. He tried to hold his hands when suddenly, the older man pulled out a gun from his back and pointed at the other man's face. I quickly stepped back a little in panic and fell hard on my back, after tangling with Chloe's harness. My arm had hit hard on a rock, and I could feel warm blood dripping from the wound. However, the pain of what I was about to witness was greater than the pain of the cut.

The younger man begged for mercy and tried to persuade the other man. I could see he was trying to reason with him and convince him to put the gun back. Did they know each other? The man with the gun grew in confidence, as he moved two steps forward toward the other. There was no way the younger one was going to survive this.

I tried to get back on my feet when a scared Chloe jumped on me from the back, making me trip on two large rocks. The sound distracted the man with the gun. He became aware that he was being watched. Just then, the man begging for mercy took advantage of the opportunity and grabbed the man by his hands. He still had the gun clutched in both his hands. Both the men now fought harder and with more force. The older man pushed the younger over the ground, where he hit his head hard on the rock. He was struggling to keep fighting but continued to hold him with his other hand. His one arm was trying to shield his face, and other was gripping the other man's arm in the air. The one on the top was stronger and more muscular. He was not ready to give up. His arm with the gun lowered dug into the other man's rib, and a loud sound of a gunshot rang through my ears. Another shooting, another man dying, I witnessed another shooting. But this one was different.

I did not know who these men were, but it felt like they knew each other well. The next thing I knew, I grabbed Chloe's harness and ran as fast as I could with the dog by my side. I kept running and did not stop to catch air. My lungs were out of breath and had started to turn dry. Breathing became difficult, as I continued to run. I realized I had peed in my pants due to the fear of being caught. I had to find my way back home, or the next dead man could be me.

I ran past thorny plants bruising my bare arms with hard ground cutting my feet. I had lost my one shoe while running and could not afford to stop and search for it. I ran till I saw the light in the distance. I followed the lights and ran further. I stopped for a minute to catch my breath. But my lungs were on fire, and the air was cutting through my windpipe, as I tried to breathe from my mouth. I started running again and ran until I reached the house, full of lights, and life. I tried to scream, but my voice was stuck in my throat. I could only feel hot air coming out of my mouth, as I tried to make a sound. I tried screaming for help, I screamed once again but fell on the ground and lost consciousness.

Chapter 3 – Part B
Loss of a Brother

Two weeks and three days had passed since I last saw my brother, I last slept with him in Grandpa's spare room, and I last saw him getting shot mercilessly by the stranger in the woods; and what did I do? I just ran away like a coward, like a scared lamb. I watched my brother die in front of my eyes and did not do anything. Every night, I lie on my bed asking myself the same questions: what could I have done to save him? Why did the monster kill him? If only I could have done something, he would be here with us, celebrating his birthday.

The house seemed unusually quiet. Mama spent most of her time in Carlo's room, going back and forth, crying, and packing his clothes for donation. She hardly left his room. Of course, her firstborn had been murdered. How she could get over this gruesome act of brutality! While she locked her emotions away in her son's room, Papa had his own way of mourning. He stayed in the basement, working long hours, and only coming out for dinner or sleep. He generally did not speak much, but it seemed like Carlo's death had made him excessively quiet and emotional. He was just quite good at hiding it. Valeri, who had always been chirpy and jumping around the house, sensed there was something wrong since nobody talked much, and everyone stayed in their own rooms. She, on several occasions, asked me where Carlo was. All I could do was look into her innocent blue eyes and lie to her face. I went downstairs to the kitchen to fix myself a meal. Mama's absence from the kitchen was evident.

The dishes were left unwashed since last night's dinner, and there was no breakfast on the table either. I poured myself some cereal and Chloe her dog biscuits. We both sat in silence and finished our meal. After we were done eating our breakfast, I washed our bowls and cleaned the kitchen. The least I could do was help Mama with some chores. As I was about to take Chloe on her usual morning walk, there was a loud knock on the door.

It was Papa's friend from the party, Consigliere Miriam Katz. The night when I witnessed Carlo's death and passed out on the front of my grandparent's house, Mr. Katz was the one who found me lying face down on the porch. He carried me inside and lay me on the sofa. After a few minutes, I woke up to find myself surrounded by the guests and my parents. Nobody had heard the gunshots and known what had happened. They all were oblivious to the fact that Carlo was missing. Papa was able to sense the tension on my face. I was sweating and panting. My eyes were filled with fear and shock. I could not find the words to utter the horrific event that I had seen. I was silent and pale like a ghost had sucked the life out of me.

"C...C...Ca...Carlo," That was all that came out of my mouth in a shaky and whispering tone.

"What about Carlo, Nico?" Asked Papa with a straight face.

He looked straight into my eyes with a cold stare, as if he knew something terrible had just happened. Suddenly, Mama was kneeling next to Papa, and her almost pleading eyes made it harder for me to say something.

"What happened, Nico? What's wrong, baby?" She asked.

"Ma...Mama," her fingers dug deeper into my arm.

"What, Nico?"

"Ca...Carlo is dead."

The words came out of my mouth, cold and lifeless. I could feel her grip loosening on my arms. There was an unusual calmness among the guests. They seemed confused and lost. Grandpa immediately began asking them to leave since the atmosphere had become intense and sorrowful.

"What do you mean he's dead?" Asked Papa, taking me by the shoulders.

"He's dead, Papa, he's dead," I repeated with tears falling down my eyes and into my mouth.

"What do you mean, Nico?" He was louder this time.

Mama sat on the floor with her head in her hands and grandma by her side. She was sobbing silently into grandma's arms.

"I... I... saw it in the woods."

"What did you see in the woods, son?" Asked Mr. Katz before Papa could inquire.

Mr. Katz stood there, calm and composed. He did not show a hint of bleakness on his face. He, along with the others, stood near the sofa. All eyes were on me, waiting for me to break the bad news.

"A man, there was a man. He shot Carlo. They were fighting, and he shot him. So, I ran. I ran fast..."

I had no idea what I was saying anymore. My words jumbled inside my mouth and made no sense. But luckily, everyone else had clearly understood what I meant. Mama's sobs grew louder. I sat there on the sofa, confused and covered in sweat and blood. I had forgotten about my bruises. The pain of losing my brother was far worse than the pain of my injuries.

Papa and Mr. Katz were out of the house and into the woods already. They did not wait for a minute and ran out in the middle of the night to hunt for my dead brother and his killer. Grandpa took out his cellphone and called the local police instantly. By this time, the guests had already left, and it was just us in the big house. Nobody said much. One of the neighbors stayed back to help us. She comforted Mama, while grandma took me to the bathroom to clean my wounds.

Fifteen minutes later, the police arrived. Two of the cops stopped by the house while others began their search in the woods. They wanted to talk to me and find out more about the scene, and what had exactly happened. I had changed my clothes and looked a lot cleaner. I was sitting on the leather recliner in the bar when one of the cops approached me. I tried my best to avoid eye contact, hoping he would leave me alone.

"You're Nico, right?" He asked, taking a seat next to me.

I silently nodded.

"I am really sorry for your loss, Nico," he tried hard to sound genuinely sorry.

"Nico, I'm Greg. I will be leading this investigation. Don't you worry, son. We'll find out who killed your brother."

He extended his hand toward me, and I took his hand. It was firm, unlike my own.

"So son, I know you're scared, but my men are out there with your father. They'll soon find out who did this. But first I need you to tell me everything that you saw, starting from the beginning."

He was now facing me. I hesitated at first, but his stern look and don't-mess-with-me face was obvious that he wanted the exact truth and nothing else. It took me precisely 10 minutes to finish my story. I was getting tired of repeating it again and again to everyone. It clearly served no purpose except bring the horrific scene back to my memory.

"Can you tell me what the killer look liked?" He inquired as I finished with my story.

"It was dark. I couldn't see," I said.

"Okay, did you hear his voice?" He further questioned.

"Yes."

"Can you tell me what did he sound like?"

"He sounded like..."

Wait! He sounded like Uncle Mike. Why did this not hit me before? I was unable to see who the man was, but I clearly remember his voice. It resembled so much like Uncle Mike's. Where was Uncle Mike now? He was not with Papa and not here. Where did he go?

"Son, can you tell me what did he sound like?" Greg asked again.

"I... I don't know," I lied.

Before the cop could ask me any more questions, the hallway was filled with loud men and Mama's sobbing. Both of us made our way to the hallway to find two policemen carrying Carlo's lifeless body. They lay the body down on the floor for us – the family to pay our last goodbyes. Papa, Mr. Katz, and Uncle Mike accompanied them. The men stood silently while Mama and grandma mourned.

Greg excused himself and took Papa to the corner of the room. They spoke in hushed voices, so I could not figure what they were talking about. After a few minutes, Mr. Katz joined them. All three of them lowered their heads and talked a little more. But my eyes were focused on one person in the entire room – Uncle Mike. He stood in the middle of the room and seemed lost.

Why would he kill Carlo? Was I wrong? But it was his voice. For a moment, I thought my mind was going to explode. The questions in my head made it difficult for me to think of anything else. I just wanted to go back home.

Papa cleared his throat and made his way to the center of the room.

"Nico, go pack your clothes and your sister's. We'll leave for home in a few hours. Miriam will stay here and help the police with the investigation," he said.

It was decided. We would go home and prepare for the burial while Mr. Katz would help the police find the killer. But, how would they ever know that the killer was one of us? He was here in this very room standing across me, and he was going to go home with me. What was I going to do with this secret inside me?

Later that night, we traveled back home in silence. The only thing that was audible was Mama's soft cries. We were told that the body would be delivered to us in four days after the forensic department would have taken samples for evidence. Uncle Mike sat in the back seat with Valeri and me. A part of me wanted to scream on top of my lungs and shake him to the core. But, another part of me was scared and had no clue what to do or who to tell.

We reached home at the dawn of the next day. Papa carried Valeri to her room, and Mama went straight to bed without saying a word. Uncle Mike and I were left behind. I did not want to be left with my brother's murderer in the same room, so I walked toward my room.

"Nico," came a husky voice from behind.

I turned around to see Uncle Mike standing behind me. He was clutching onto his bag of clothes. He looked rough and worn out as if he had not slept for days. None of us had slept for days, but he looked worse.

"Can we talk... please..." he asked.

Although being in his presence was the last thing I wanted, I quietly walked down the stairs, facing him.

"What?"

My face was red. I threw the words in his face as blatantly as I could.

"What's with the attitude, son?" He caught me by the arm.

"Let go of me."

I pulled myself away from him. I stood there with a red face and rage in my eyes.

"Look, Nico. I just want to know what you told the police. We all are upset about Carlo's death, but we have to be here for each other," he said.

"I told them the truth," I said, feeling proud of myself.

"What truth, Nico?" He asked again.

I could see the tension building up on his face. His muscles had begun to tighten. I decided to remain quiet and watch him suffer for a few minutes like he left my brother alone to suffer in the cold night.

"Please, Nico. I'm sorry for whatever happened. He was my blood too. I am equally sorry for whatever happened to him but look, don't you worry. After Carlo, you're the one who's gonna take care of the business. It'll just be your father, you, and me."

He stood there, waiting for me to reply. How could this man talk about blood? He had killed his own nephew. My insides were on fire.

"I don't care about the business," I screamed and pushed him aside.

"Young boy, you're being absolutely ridiculous now," he yelled.

"What's happening here?" Came a voice from behind.

It was Papa standing near the basement door. I stood there in silence, wondering what to respond.

"Nothing, Marco. Nico and I were just talking about how he would be taking over the business soon."

The words flowed through him without any effort.

"Okay," said Papa. *"Mike, come with me, we need to talk."*

The two men stayed there for one long hour, while I sat at the dining table petting Chloe. Since the incident night, I had not paid much attention to her. She missed Carlo and slept with his slippers tucked under her head like a pillow.

After an hour, Uncle Mike walked out of the room with a big smile on his face, and his chest broadened. He looked unusually happy about something unknown to me.

"Uncle Mike, what happened? You look happy."

"Well, your Papa has just handed me half of the operations of the business. Since Carlo is not with us anymore, someone has to take over his part. And Marco thinks I'm the best guy. Don't worry, young man. Our family business is in safe hands," he boasted.

He muttered his last words and walked away from me. He just walked away from my family, robbing us of our business, my brother, and my parents' son. The investigation was in the process. The police were still not able to find the murderer. Of course, he had not left any trace. He had just fled. I let him escape. Greg, the cop, who interrogated me, was replaced by Mr. Katz.

This is why he went back and forth from San Francisco to Virginia City. This was his third visit in the last two weeks. He and Papa spent long hours in the basement, discussing the case and its progress. I never got a chance to speak to Mr. Katz since we left Virginia City. We only passed greetings from a distance.

Today, we were alone, and I was hoping I would get a chance to talk to him myself before Papa or anyone else could discover.

"How are you doing, son?" He extended his hands toward me.

"I'm good sir, thank you," I replied in the most polite manner.

"How's your mother doing?" He inquired.

"She's good too, sir."

Mr. Katz seemed pleased with my answers. He was a tall man who wore a long black coat and a tilted coachman bowler's hat. He had gray mustaches and dark-filled eyebrows. He must be 6 feet 2 inches tall, slightly taller and muscular than Papa. He had a unique appearance to his personality. He was older, maybe in his early 60s but looked a lot younger for his age. He walked straight with his back arched and possessed manners of a military person.

"Is your father again in the basement?" He asked in his hoarse voice.

"Yes, sir," I replied with my eyes lowered.

"Alright then, I'll go talk to him."

As Mr. Katz walked toward the basement door, I reached out for him and grabbed him by the arm.

"Sir!"

"Yes, son. Is everything okay?" He asked in bewilderment.

"Yes... Yes sir, can I talk to you for a minute?" I asked hesitatingly.

"Sure, son, what do you want to talk about?"

His eyes were piercing into my soul.

"I... I want you to stop the investigation," I managed to blurt the words out.

They seemed icy cold in my throat. A part of me felt like I had betrayed my older brother.

"Stop the investigation? What do you mean, son?"

He looked more confused than ever.

"I know this may sound absurd coming from a 15-year-old, but sir, I really need you to stop the investigation," I persisted.

"And why do you want me to do that, child?"

"Carlo and I may not be that close, but he was my older

brother. I loved him, and I feel the investigation is not helping my family in any way. I can't see my mom crying in his room all night. I can't see my father locked away in the basement, taking out all his frustration on his work."

I took a short pause before speaking again.

"I want my family to get back normal again. What's done is done, sir. We don't want any more of this misery."

"But, don't you want justice for your brother's murder? Don't you want to know who killed him and why?" He asked.

How did I tell him that I already knew who the murderer was and for the sake of my family, I was tongue-tied? How did I say to him that Carlo's murderer was his own uncle?

"No, sir. I think my family's better off without knowing who killed their oldest son. It will only add more to our sorrow."

"Does your father know about this, Nico?" He leaned in closer to me.

"No, sir. But I am begging you to stop this investigation. Please, if you don't stop this investigation, there could be severe consequences for my family."

"Be careful what you wish for, son."

"I know what I'm wishing for, sir."

"For a 15-year-old, you think and talk like an adult. Make your father proud, Nico," he patted my shoulder.

That's exactly what I am doing, Mr. Katz, I thought to myself.

"Now, I'll go talk to your father, and you stay out of trouble, young boy."

"Will do," I replied.

I am sorry, Carlo. Hope you forgive me. I was not able to do justice to your murder. I let your killer walk away. Papa gave him half of the business that belonged to you. You deserved better, big brother. I'm sorry… I don't know what to do. Tears flowed through my eyes, as I thought to myself and cried.

Chapter 4
Realization

"Nico, come down, I'm waiting," yelled Papa from down the hall.

I rubbed my eyes, swept the blanket from my body, and made my way to the bathroom, all at the same time. This was the second time Papa had called out for me. It is better to hurry up before he comes upstairs fuming with anger. Lately, I had been sleeping a lot. Luca was generous in offering me some weed for free. At first, I was hesitant, not sure if I should be doing it, but then I thought to myself, 'W*ho cares!'* I have to be honest, I never thought it would feel so good, so relieving, so relaxing, and so out of this world.

Although I was very cautious of hiding it under my bed in a box of my action figures collection, I feared Mama would figure out while cleaning my room. Not that I worried about what she would think, I just did not want to send another anguish to her way when she was not yet over her oldest son's death. Everything had gone back to normal. I do not know what Mr. Katz said to Papa, but it appeared like the investigation into Carlo's murder was over.

Mr. Katz had gone back to Virginia City, whereas Papa and Uncle Mike had gotten involved in breaking deals in their business. Papa had stopped talking about the tragedy that hit our family three months back. I do not think he was immune to grief, but he was great at pretending. For me, I had learned new coping mechanisms, although unhealthy, yet very satisfying. I spent more time with Luca at the back of the school ground, smoking pot and making out with hot girls. My grades were good like they always had been, so no one really thought about my ability to turn into a rebel.

However, the only person for whom things had not gone back to normal was my mother. There were days when she would come out of her room and make Carlo's favorite food in the kitchen. There were also days when she would lock herself in her room, along with Valerie, and refuse to come out until Papa came home late at night. He did not complain much. However, I feared he would soon have an outbreak if she continued mourning over her dead son.

"Coming, Papa."

I screamed from the bathroom, as I splashed cold water on my face, trying to hide the tiredness in my eyes. I grabbed a dirty T-shirt from the laundry basket and put it over my head as I walked out of the room and down the stairs.

"How long were you going to make me wait, Nico?" Asked Papa with a stern face.

"I'm sorry. I slept late last night. I was studying in my room," I lied with a straight face.

Somehow I felt nothing anymore. Lying came naturally to me. I had stopped trying to be the perfect son when I realized I was really not one.

"Alright, now hurry up. We're running late," he said as he walked in front of me toward the door.

After Mr. Katz left for Virginia City, Papa had invited me to his office in the basement for the first time. I was confused and shocked. The basement was for business purposes strictly. The only people who were invited to his office were Mr. Katz, Uncle Mike, and Carlo. Papa asked me to take a seat in front of him, and I quietly obeyed. What came after was something I had been expecting since Carlo's death. However, I was not ready for it, at least not so soon.

"Nico, when does school get off for summer vacations?" He asked.

"In two weeks, Papa," I replied as I moved my eyes across the room, inspecting the unorganized files and papers lying unattended at his desk.

"Hmm..." He arched his back and sat straight in his leather recliner with his arms in front of him on the desk. *"Nico, since your brother is not with us anymore, I want you to take his place in the business with me,"* He said as plainly as he could.

It was funny how he referred to Carlo as my brother and not his son. I have to agree, as compared to my mother, my father was way too good at hiding his emotions, especially in front of the people who you call your family.

"But... Papa, I have plans to go camping with Luca," I protested politely.

To be honest, I was not sure if I was going to camp this summer. I was thinking to spend most of my time at Luca's place, smoking pot, playing video games, and making out with random girls from the internet.

"Not this summer, Nico. You're not a kid anymore. It's time for you to learn about our family business. You're old enough to take responsibility. And you will start with me and Uncle Mike this summer."

"Uncle Mike?" I asked, stunned.

"Yes, is there a problem?"

He raised his eyebrows as he looked straight at me from the opposite side.

"Yes, there is a problem, Papa. A big problem. Your brother killed your son," I screamed on the inside, knowing that I will never be able to blurt the words out loud.

"Nico, I asked you. Is there any problem?" He asserted.

"No... No, Papa, there's no problem at all."

I tried to avoid eye contact.

"Good, get out of here. We'll begin training you in a few weeks."

***

We had been driving for twenty minutes now when Papa finally stopped the car in a different part of the city. There were hardly any people out on the streets. Some women were sitting outside their houses, rocking their babies in their laps while speaking in hushed voices. At a distance, few men were dressed in white vests and ripped blue jeans, smoking what I thought were cigarettes and playing loud music from the stereos.

It seemed like a poor neighborhood. The houses were made with red bricks and were in bad condition. Most of the houses were painted red, white, and gray. The children played outside of their houses with abandoned furniture and flat tires. There was a weird feeling about this place. The people looked scared and mysterious. They looked at us in a bizarre way, as we did not belong here. There was a small bar at the end of the street called The Bronze Drink. I thought people visited there at night on weekends, but there were men and women walking out of the bar in broad daylight on a Monday.

We stopped in front of an old garage that was painted gray in some areas and vandalized with yellow spray paint on other areas. The empty patches of paint were proof that the building had been in this place for many years, and no one really maintained it. The windows were broken, and wild plants grew from under the damp ground. The site, in general, was very spooky. There was a broken yet functional payphone outside the garage, and a few cars parked outside at a distance.

"Come on in, Nico," Papa motioned at me to follow him inside of the old and rusted garage.

I followed him inside the garage. It was mostly dark, except a few places that were lit by yellow luminescent lamps. The inside of it resembled a detention center I saw in one of the old movies at Luca's home. I thought it was just going to be Papa and me, but there were a couple of other men in the garage too. Most of them did not notice us walking in. A few came forward to greet Papa. They also shook hands with me. I have to admit, as much as I was loathing this place, I appreciated the attention I was receiving.

We continued to walk toward a table with two empty seats that were located in the middle of the room. Papa took the seat in front, and I sat on the one opposite him. Not sure if it was ever going to be the right time for me to ask questions, I quickly jumped to the point.

"Is this where you work, Papa?" I asked enthusiastically.

"Hmm..." he nodded as he dug into a pile of papers in front of him.

I spent the next few minutes looking across the room at the empty cardboard boxes stacked up against the wall and the men, along with a few young boys of my age, working their way through. They kept their heads down and worked without moving an inch. There was another man, much older than the rest who walked back and forth, keeping an eye on the young boys. He was taller and had a look about him that made you fear him. I think the boys felt the same.

Papa raised his eyes from the papers in front of him, as Uncle Mike approached him.

"I see you brought Nico today, big brother," he said loudly in an unusually quiet place.

"Yes, Mike. I figured it's time for him to get involved in the business," Papa replied.

I watched quietly as my father and uncle – also my brother's murderer – sat in front of me to talk about business in a language that seemed so foreign to me.

After almost 10 minutes, Papa looked at me and said, *"Nico, Uncle Mike will show you around and tell you how the place is actually run, okay."*

"Why Uncle Mike? Why can't you show me around, Papa?"

I needed every possible reason to stay away from Uncle Mike.

"What's wrong with your Uncle showing you around, son?" He asked, inquisitively.

Disappointed, I looked down at my feet and whispered an almost audible, *"Nothing,"*

"Good, I'll be out for the day, running around. You boys, have fun."

He patted on Uncle Mike's shoulder and left with a big smile. I could clearly see on Papa's face how excited and happy he was to have me at his workplace. I wasn't going to burst his bubble, but this was not the most idealistic workplace. Not the kind of work I ever wanted to do, yet here I was making up for my dead brother. Did I receive this position in inheritance, or was it just fate?

"So, young man, you ready for the tour?" Uncle Mike asked with a smirk.

'Sure..." I replied with the same smirk.

We walked toward the end of the garage, where two middle-aged men sat talking on cell phones and thick black leather diaries in front of them.

"Mario, amico mio, come stai," He greeted the man on the right in Italian and embraced him in a big hug.

"Mikkie, grande mamma, è Bello vederti!" He greeted him with the same enthusiasm.

"Mario, meet Nico, Marco's son. It's his first day at work," he introduced me as if I was his prized trophy.

The bearded men extended their hands toward me. I shook hands politely with a smile on my face.

"Your brother was a good boss. We all miss him very much. But it's good to know you'll be joining us. It's going to be an honor working with you, sir." said Mario with a fading smile.

"Call me Nico, please," I said.

"Shall we move on then?" Interrupted Uncle Mike. *"Don't want to bore him on his first day of work."*

We moved forward from the corner to the middle of the room. Since Papa was not there, I was not hesitant to ask questions.

"What is their job?" I asked Uncle Mike, pointing to the two men we just left behind.

"Well, they keep things running smoothly. They call up different businesses in the town and let them know we'll be paying them a visit. They're like the welcoming committee."

I could feel his grip on my shoulder tightening.

"And you see those two men, Nico?" He asked, pointing at the door where two 6' 2" tall men were standing. They had massive bodies, just like those I saw in the wrestling. They stood straight with their backs arched and their eyes fixed on the door of the garage.

"Yes," I replied.

"Their job is to make sure we get the money and the shipment safely."

"What shipment?" I asked, confused.

"You know, all sorts of stuff and the likes..." He said casually with a wide smile on his emotionless face.

"Drugs...?" I asked in shock.

Uncle Mike didn't answer.

"You see those young boys there," he pointed to the group of boys almost my age. *"They live nearby. Your father and I actually help them and their families. They come to us asking for work, Nico. Their job is to pack boxes with merchandise and deliver them to the other side of the town safely."*

"I didn't know we shipped things," I said in a disappointing tone.

"You don't know a lot of things, Nico."

Uncle Mike stood facing me in the middle of the room. The yellow light made his facial lines more visible. He was in his late thirties and unmarried. However, no one could deny his numerous affairs. One could clearly tell he was not aging gracefully.

"But, I know a lot of things about you, Uncle Mike," I asserted.

"What do you mean, Nico?" His expressions straightened.

"I know your secret, Uncle Mike. I know you."

"Mike, Nico," came a familiar voice from behind.

"Papa," I exclaimed and moved forward to greet my father, leaving uncle behind. He followed.

"Nico, your mother called. She is preparing dinner today. We better hurry to reach home in time before its dark. The weather is quite unpredictable in this part of the town."

"Mike, come with us and have dinner."

Papa invited his son's murderer to his home for dinner yet again. I could not really blame my father for something he did not know. But what triggered me was why he could not see through him. He could not see his awfulness through his disgusting face. More than that, how good Uncle Mike was at hiding it. Before leaving, Papa exchanged a few words with the tall, muscular men and handed them some keys. The ride back home was silent. Uncle Mike sat in the passenger seat, humming to some music. I was this close to revealing his secret to him, but luckily for him, Papa interrupted me. In all reality, he owed me big time, considering I saved his ass.

***

The house smelled good today. The aroma of rosemary and fermented lemons filled our nostrils. The place was cleaned. The chandelier that was only turned on for special occasions was shining brighter than the moon outside. Valerie sat in front of the television, watching Looney Toons, while Mama walked around the kitchen gracefully. The sight of her cooking, doing her most favorite thing in the world, was more soothing than the first puff of weed. She wore her favorite cotton dress, embroidered with lilies and white lotus. Just as much as I appreciated this sight of her working in her kitchen, my father was even more elevated at seeing his wife in her happy place.

All five of us took our places at the table. I have to be honest that it felt a holiday. However, I was also confused at what had triggered this sudden change of mood in my mother, yet I dared not ask in fear of her going falling back into her misery. The table was decorated with several dishes – our family's traditional roasted chicken with mashed potatoes, stir-fried vegetables, bolognas spaghetti, and apple pies. We all sat in silence and devoured our meal. It was too delicious for us to distract ourselves with unnecessary conversation. But, apparently, that was not what Uncle Mike believed in.

"Marie, this food is divine," he said with a mouthful while waiving his fork around like he was conducting an orchestra.

Mama continued to eat her meal and refused to respond.

He greedily poured some more gravy into his already loaded plate. I could not believe the fact that the murderer of my brother was sitting at our table, among us, enjoying the meal. I dug my fork angrily in the piece of chicken lying untouched on my plate.

"Why aren't you eating your meal, Nico?" Papa noticed.

"He's probably had a rough first day, Marco," chuckled

Uncle Mike as he answered on my behalf.

"Is that so, Nico?" Papa intervened.

"No, Papa," I replied in two words.

"Why don't you tell us all about your first day, Nico," interrupted Uncle Mike again.

I did not reply.

"Answer your Uncle, Nico," Papa said.

"It was fine," I said as I was forced to talk.

Papa could sense the tension in the dining room, but he continued to enjoy his meal.

"Your son is gonna have a lot more fun days, brother," said Uncle Mike gulping the red wine down his throat.

"I don't want to be a part of the family business, Papa," I said abruptly without thinking of the consequences.

The clinking of Papa's fork with his plate echoed in the silent room.

"What do you mean you don't want to be a part of the business? Haven't I made it pretty clear? After your brother, it's you who has to look after it."

"Yea, Nico, what do you mean you don't want to be a part

of the business?" Said Uncle Mike, who was now getting on my nerves.

"I don't want to be a part the filthy business that my family is a part of, Papa," I said, as I fought back the tears from flowing out of my eyes.

"Nico, do you know what you are saying?" Said Uncle Mike.

"You stay out of this, Uncle Mike," I banged my fist hard on the table. The loud noises and the banging scared Valerie, who started crying. *"I know what you have done to our family."*

The tears flowed freely.

"Enough," yelled Papa. *"Nico, get up and go to your room. Don't test me, boy,"* his face was red with anger. I knew I had to obey him before fueling his anger anymore. *"You are grounded for the rest of the summer, you understand?"* He yelled from behind.

My dinner plate left untouched. I quietly stood up and walked up to my room without saying another word.

Chapter 5
Revenge Taken

"I only need $200, Luca," I enunciated my words with my hands in the air.

"Yeah, and I ask you for what? You're grounded, not like you can leave the house anyway. I don't charge you for the pot, so what do you need that much money for?"

Luca took a long puff of smoke and released it in the air. The smoke created perfectly rounded hoops, disappearing into thin air.

"I can't tell you that," I lowered my voice.

"Well then, you can't have the money."

"Urgh..." I made a loud groaning sound.

"Why don't you ask your dad for the money?" He asked.

"Huh," I groaned, putting my green stripes T-shirt over my head. *"You think it's that easy? He would ask me a hundred questions, 'What do you want to do with it, Nico?' 'What you are gonna spend it on?' and I don't wanna answer them."*

"To be honest, I'm a bit worried too. You're kinda acting very strange, man!" Luca said, standing up from my unmade bed. *"Here, you can have the money, but I want it back, or I'll tell your Papa about it."*

He imitated the way I usually said *Papa* and laughed it off with a smirk on his face.

"Thanks, man! I promise I'll return it."

I thanked him with a one-armed hug and a single backslap. He hated it.

"By the way, are you and Marie Ann a thing?" I asked hesitatingly.

Marie Ann was our new classmate who had transferred her school from Detroit when her parents got divorced. She had tanned skin, blue eyes, and short dark curls that traced the structure of her rounded face. She was different than other girls of our age.

She played sports, ate greasy food, got straight A's, wore the prettiest dresses, and had the most honeyed voice. All the boys in the class grew a crush on her when she had first joined the school. She remained the talk of the school for the next few weeks that followed. I admit that my fascination for Sophie slowly died when Luca and I became friends with

Marie. I secretly had feelings for her, too but was too shy to make a move. I was hoping to tell her over the summer, but due to the turn of events and my sad family situation, I lost the little confidence that I thought I had. What was worse was that I found out Luca had been hanging out with her a little too much while I had been locked up in my house.

"Why do you ask that?" He raised an eyebrow.

"No reason." I shrugged. *"I know you like her too, and I know you've been hanging out with her a lot recently."*

"Yeah, but that does not mean we are a thing unless you like her too, Nico," he retaliated. *"Is that why you need the $200 to take her out on a date?"* He smirked again.

"Hahahaha ... Nah man, it's for something else," I assured him.

"Okay okay ... Anyway, I gotta go and hit the road, and you, my friend, need to get out of the house soon. It's messing you up," Luca said as he hinted toward the mess I had made in my room and maybe my life, I guess.

"Take care, Lu," I called out from my room as he walked out of it.

Luca was right. Staying inside the home for just a week had messed me up and my thoughts. There were times when I would walk into Carlo's room and spend hours while Mama and Papa slept in their room. I did not know why I did that, but I would stay there for hours, going through his stuff, the action figures that he would not let me borrow, and finally fall asleep on his bed. I was too embarrassed to be found on his bed in the morning, so I would wake up around 5 a.m. and quietly walk back to my room.

Just as much as I could not stop thinking about Carlo, I could also not stop thinking about Uncle Mike, and how he was the reason behind my family's misery. My parents were unaware of the fact, but I knew it. I knew it all in vain! I was unable to put aside the thoughts of stopping Mr. Katz from investigating Carlo's murder. Of course, he kept my secret, but that made me question my love for my brother.

Was I deceiving my blood? Was I just going to let the murderer of my brother get away with it? The guilt was now seeping into my body, infiltrating every cell, and every thought. I knew I had to do something about it. But what? I remembered I had to take Valeri for dance class, which was my only escape these days and a part of my punishment that Papa had given me.

I quickly got dressed and went downstairs. He was seated at the table, eating some pasta before leaving for work.

"You're late. Your sister has been waiting for 20 minutes for you to take her," he said without taking his eyes off his plate.

I looked around and saw Mama watching the TV while Valerie sat all dressed up beside her, waiting for me.

"I ... I was getting dressed, Papa."

"Hmm..." Papa murmured.

I moved toward the living room to take Valerie, who was already jumping with excitement. I took her hand, and we both made our way outside of the house when Papa called out for me.

"Nico!"

"Yes, Papa?"

I stopped and turned back.

"Come here," he ordered.

With Valerie on my side, we both stood in front of Papa, while he sat at the dining table. He was done eating, and Mama had picked up the empty plates.

"Nico, as much as I dislike the way you acted with your uncle last week over dinner. I have decided to end your punishment. But, that does not mean you get to repeat such a thing again. Do you get it?"

"Yes, Papa," I obediently nodded, even though I knew I was going to oppose him soon.

"Now take your sister to dance class and come back soon, both of you. We'll have dinner together as a family."

***

You can tell Mama had put all her efforts in making this dinner special. This was the first dinner we were having as a family. I know we had dinner last week, but since that included Uncle Mike, I did not really consider that a successful family dinner. This one was different. It was Papa, Mama, Valerie, and me. Carlo's seat remained empty.

Of course, we could never be a complete family without him, but I guess everyone had begun to move on. Even Mama had started wearing her favorite dresses, making all her favorite food, and was surprisingly in a good mood too. However, were they able to stop their thoughts, or was this a show? Because I clearly could not. The more I tried not to think about Carlo, the guiltier I felt.

Mama made pot roast, with mashed potatoes, quinoa salad, and bread rolls. As usual, it was incredibly satisfying food. I was almost finished eating what was on my plate when Papa asked me to meet him in his basement office after dinner. I finished after him, so he was already in the basement, waiting for me. I did not want to keep him waiting for too long, so I quickly finished, washed my hands, and made my way downstairs to his office.

"Papa, can I come in?" I knocked on the mahogany door.

"Nico, come on in, son."

He motioned me toward the chair in front of him. I sat patiently, waiting for him to break the ice.

"Son, look. I know that your brother's death has taken a toll on you. We're all suffering in our own ways. But that doesn't mean we turn our backs on family. Mike is your uncle, Nico. He feels sad about Carlo's death as much as we do. He is family. I want you to treat him like it."

He paused for a few seconds.

"Son, after your brother's death, there is a lot of responsibility on you. You're not a young boy anymore. You have to take care of this family. You have to take care of our family business as well."

He finished speaking and leaned back in the chair, waiting for me to respond.

"What if I don't want to do this, Papa?"

"This is the family business, Nico. You don't have an option. Your brother was going to continue doing this, and so would you, son," he said sternly.

"But..."

Before I could protest anymore, Papa's phone started ringing. He excused himself and moved out of the room to answer. I was filled with rage. How can my father decide what I do with my life? Should that not be my decision to make? Should I not have a say in this? If only Papa knew, he is calling his son's murderer, family.

I angrily banged my hand on the table. It hit hard, even harder than it should have on a wooden table. I moved away from the newspapers, only to find a shiny black gun on his desk. It looked new. I did not know my father owned a gun until today. I wondered why he had it in the first place.

I carefully picked up the gun in my hands. It was not the first time I had held a gun, this one was heavier. It glowed in the luminescent lights of the basement.

The door opened, and Papa came in. I instantly put the gun back where it was kept, hoping he did not notice me playing with his gun.

"So, where was I?" He asked.

"It's okay, Papa. I get what you're saying. I'll do as you say. I'll help you run the family business."

"You will?"

"Yes, Papa!"

"Good boy, Nico! That's all I require of you. There has been a lot going on at work. We've got a big shipment coming tomorrow, and all the employees are on holidays. It's just your Uncle Mike and me. Some days, it gets really exhausting. Carlo was a lot of help. We all miss him, son," he said, taking a deep breath.

"Papa, if it's okay with you, I can help Uncle Mike receive the shipment tomorrow."

I offered.

"You sure, you're ready for it?" He asked.

I nodded in reply.

"Perfect, then. Even I think it's time you start taking some

big steps," he said as he sat straight in his leather recliner.

"I'll let Mike know that you're coming," he said with a smile on his face. *"Now, go off and sleep. You'd have to wake up early to leave for the garage."*

"Yes," I stood up from the chair as discreetly as possible.

"But, wait ... how do you plan on going? You do realize it's a long ride?" He asked as I walked toward the door.

"Don't worry, Papa. I have some money. I'll use that to travel to the other side of the town."

I was confident.

"Okay, then. Good night, Nico."

"Good night, Papa."

***

It was a beautiful morning. I could hear the birds chirping outside my window. The news reporter on last night's news had said that it would probably rain today, and I hoped he was right. I could not sleep much the whole night. I rolled in my bed, trying to fight the thoughts of Carlo's pain and the brutal death he experienced, which he did not even deserve. I also realized that I was sweating more than usual. The adrenaline and the anxiety were building up.

I had planned to eat a good breakfast, so I could maintain a stomach for the events of the day. It was already a good day. I hoped it ended the same way. The clock on my wall struck 7 a.m., I heard Mama's footsteps outside of my bedroom, walking toward the kitchen. That was basically the routine. Every day she woke up, got dressed, and made her way to the kitchen to do her favorite thing in the world – cooking.

I was lucky. I found a clean T-shirt in my closet. I paired it up with a pair of blue denim jeans and my old red and white sneakers. I put extra effort into making my hair and made sure they looked sleek. I do not remember the last time I took a good look at myself in the mirror and put this much time in getting ready. Today, indeed, it was a special day.

I walked downstairs to the kitchen where Papa was already seated reading the daily newspaper with a bowl of cereal in front of him. Mama was standing next to the stove, making blueberry pancakes – the same ones she usually makes for my birthday.

"Good morning, Papa. Good morning, Mama," I greeted with excitement.

"Good morning, Nico," said Papa putting his newspaper aside and taking a spoon full of his cereal.

Mama put a plate of pancakes in front of me with some maple syrup and honey. She knew how I liked my breakfast and made sure I ate before I started the big day.

"So, are you prepared, Nico? It could be a long day at work, so eat up." Papa said.

"Yes, Papa. I'm really excited to start work today."

"You see that brown envelope?"

He pointed toward a brown package lying on top of the table in the living room.

"Give that to Mike. He'll know what to do with it. Be careful with it, Nico. It's important."

"Yes, Papa," I nodded enthusiastically.

Soon Mama joined us, and we continued to eat our breakfast in silence.

After breakfast, Papa, as usual, made his way to the basement, while I wore my backpack after carefully placing the package inside it. The bus for the other side of the town would soon be leaving, so I hurried and ran to the nearest bus stop.

I waited for approximately 15 minutes when the first bus came. I hopped on to it and grabbed the first empty seat I could find. The bus was not really crowded, which gave me more time to think and reassess my decisions. I knew I was doing the right thing. I was going to make it all right. Papa was right – this is *our* family business. And I will, at all cost, protect it and fight for it, just like Carlo did.

It took me 45 minutes to reach the other side of the town. It was unusually quiet than the last time I had been here. However, I had still not reached my destination. The bus dropped me at the only bus stop in the area, which was located in a distant part of the town. I walked for another 10 minutes when I finally reached the garage. I tried opening it when I realized it was already open. Apparently, Uncle Mike had shown up earlier.

I ducked from under the shutter into the dark, oddly smelling garage. There was not a single man in sight, except Uncle Mike sitting on the same chair that Papa sat on when he first brought me to this place. Watching him sit in the same chair made me furious. I could sense the rage building up inside me already. I hated him more and more each day. I could not wait for that feeling to go away.

"Nico!" He yelled from across the room, waving his hand to guide me.

"Hey," I replied as flatly as I could.

"Marcus told me that you'd be coming to receive the shipment with me. I want you to know that we're very proud of you, Nico. Your brother would have been proud of you too," he said as he patted my shoulder with his hand.

How dare he talk about my brother like that? Who gives him the right to talk about my brother when he was the one who killed him? I thought to myself.

I quickly shrugged his hand from my shoulder and stepped back.

"What's wrong, Nico? Why are you acting so strange?" He inquired.

I grew angry. My eyes had become blood-red, and my fists were clenching while my teeth gritted under my breath.

"I know you killed my brother," I finally let the cat out of the bag.

"What?" He exclaimed in disbelief.

"I was there, Uncle Mike. I watched you kill my brother. I watched how you brutally killed my brother!" I screamed

the words in his face.

"I'm pretty sure you're mistaken, kid," he said as if he had become immune to the ugly deed he committed. I could feel warm tears building up in my eyes. I tried hard to fight them back.

"You're a fuckin' liar. I watched how you did it. I was there behind the tree. I watched it all."

I was louder this time. There was a moment's silence. We both stared at each other without saying a word. He made his way back to the chair where he was sitting before. He leaned back, crossed his legs, and looked straight at me.

"You know what? I actually did kill your brother. And you want to know why little Nico?" He said confidently with a smirk.

A part of me did not want to hear why, but the other part was dying to know what made him kill his nephew. So I simply stood there without answering him.

"I did kill him, Nico, because he was getting in my way. He was taking what rightfully belonged to me. First, it was your father, and then it was going to be his sons. I could not let that happen. I was supposed to have all the rights to the business, but your father got it all. He was good. He was

better than everyone I ever knew. Everyone respected him, while I was just an underdog, following his orders like a fool. Then he brought your brother into the business. All my chances of owning it faded with your brother coming in. So, I had to get him out of my way. You see, I was actually going to spare his life, but that rat had a big mouth. He figured that I had already transferred most of the funds in my own name, and he was going to rat me out. So I decided to kill him and my secret with him." He said without any remorse.

"You're an evil man," I replied.

He smiled, got up from the chair, and walked toward the mini refrigerator.

"You know, given that now you know my secret too, that means I might have to kill you too."

He got himself a beer from the fridge and turned back to face me.

"Not before I kill you first, Uncle Mike."

I stood there, pointing the heavy metallic gun at him that I had stolen from Papa's basement office.

"Woah! Nico! Where did you get that from?" He was shocked.

"Doesn't matter. I'm here to kill you like you murdered Carlo."

"Nico, give that gun to me."

He placed his beer bottle on the table and walked hesitatingly toward me with his hands in the air enunciating his words.

"Step back!" I yelled louder than ever.

"Okay ... okay, Nico, relax. I'm sure there's a better way we can talk this out." He pleaded just like Carlo did for his life. *"You don't even know how to use a gun, dammit."*

His forehead was clouded with sweat droplets. His voice was shaky. I could clearly see the panic on his face, and how badly he wanted this moment to end.

"Actually, I do. In fact, I've used it before, and I am not afraid to use it again on you." I said confidently.

"Nico, please think about it. I'm your uncle for God's sake."

"And he was your nephew, your own blood, dammit."

My anger was reaching its peak. I wanted to get done with this immediately. Yet, he took advantage of the opportunity and tried to pry the gun away from my hands. His grip was tight. My fingers, between his hands, pressed harder at the gun's metallic body.

"Let go, Nico," he said from under his teeth.

I was not going to give up. I was going to put up a bigger fight than he expected. We continued to fight. Going back and forth, his body was a lot heavier than mine. He was also a lot stronger than me. There was no way I could dominate him. But I knew it was now or never. The image of the night when Carlo died replayed in my mind so vividly. The way he begged for his life, the way he fought for what was right but was silenced kept recurring in my mind like a bad memory.

But this was not the time to think about them. I tried to push the thoughts out of my mind. I tried hard. The trigger was pulled, and the bullets were fired. The smoke from the gun's nozzle spiraled in the air. The loud noise of the gun echoed in the empty garage. A thud of someone falling on the floor was heard. A pool of blood gathered on the dirty garage floor. Someone was killed.

Chapter 6
The Regret

I woke up with a headache from last night. The sunshine was bright in my room. I loved the previous day, but I hated the present day. I arched my arm over my eyes to block the sunlight, but it did not help. After minutes of struggling to find the right position in bed, I woke up feeling irritated. I was unable to put the thoughts out of my head. The loud crack of the bullet rang in my ears repeatedly. My forehead was covered with sweat. It was an unusually hot day, I thought.

My clothes lay beside the bed, dirty and stinking. I obviously could not put them in the laundry. They needed to be thrown away immediately. That reminded me that I was stinking too. Perhaps, a cold shower would help me. So, I headed to take a shower. Soon, I got out of the shower, panting and anxious. It was not a good start of the day. I thought if I skipped breakfast and went over to Luca's place, it would help keep my mind occupied and away from Papa and Mama's eyes. But, Luca had gone to visit his grandparents, so I had nowhere else to go.

I quietly made my way downstairs trying not to make a sound, hoping there was no one in the hall so it would be easier for me to sneak out. But fate had different plans for me. The house was crowded with men in uniform. I panicked, clenched my fists, and turned around to go back to my room.

"Nico!" Came a voice from behind.

"Shit ... did they find out it was me?" I thought to myself.

I turned around to see Mama standing near the end of the stairs, staring right through me.

"Son, come down. We have to tell you something," she said in a sad voice.

"Mama ... uhm ... what's the police doing in our house? What happened?" I asked.

"Nico, somebody killed Uncle Mike ..." She said with tears in her eyes.

I was unsure of how to react. I tried my best to hide my face. I could not offer my sympathy, so I simply asked where Papa was. She pointed to the living room where he was seated between two police officers. One of them was black, who was taking notes while the white policeman was asking

Papa questions. Papa looked devastated. His head was buried in his hands. I walked toward them dubiously and stood near the sofa in the living room, waiting for them to notice me. It was a flashback to the same night when Carlo died, and my grandparents' house was filled with cops. They questioned us the same way they did that day. There was no running from the memories that kept coming back to me.

Soon this would be over too, and we all would forget Uncle Mike. However, if this was all for good, then why was I regretting it? Why were there feelings of shame and guilt seeping through my lungs? It should have been liberating, free from all threads, but here I was, feeling suffocated, and wanting to run away.

"No, Nico! You're not a coward like your uncle. You avenged your brother's death. You did the right thing," I assured myself.

My thoughts were interrupted with Papa calling my name.

"Nico, son, come here," he called out.

I moved forward.

"Papa," was all I could murmur.

"Somebody killed your uncle last night, Nico."

Papa's voice was breaking, yet he was trying his best to maintain himself.

"Yes, Papa. I know," I replied, feeling sorry for my father, not for my uncle.

Papa took a deep breath and a long pause before saying anything else.

"Nico," he looked sideways before continuing. *"Since you were the last person your uncle met, the police want to ask you a few questions. I know it's hard for you, son, but you have to answer them, so they can find the killer as soon as possible."*

"Yes, Papa, it is fine. I understand."

Papa was replaced with me between the two men. He went to talk to the other men standing across the room.

"Young man, we're really sorry for your loss. But, we need to ask you a few questions that could help us solve your uncle's murder," the white policemen said.

I started sweating again. That reminded me of the time when the policeman had questioned me in Virginia City. I had lied then and would lie today too.

"Nico, that's your name, right?"

"Yes, sir," I said as I looked at my hands.

"Nico, can you tell us what time did you meet your uncle yesterday?"

I genuinely tried to remember the time but had no recollection of this particular detail.

"I ... I don't remember. It was midday, I guess."

"Okay, and where did you meet him?"

"At my father's warehouse."

"Can you tell us what happened there, son?" Said the black policeman on the left.

I took a small pause before starting with my lie.

"I had gone there to get the shipment with Uncle Mike," I said in a boyish tone.

My story has to be well crafted. I could not afford to give myself away, I thought.

"Uncle Mike was already there, waiting for me. He knew that I was coming. I met him inside the garage. We both sat and waited for the shipment to arrive. After a few hours, the shipment came. We received and checked it. It was fine, but

Uncle Mike was constantly getting phone calls. He looked a little upset."

I took a few more minutes to come up with the second half of the story.

"After we got the shipment, he said he wanted me to leave urgently. I told him that I would stay and help him with it, but he said he would do it himself. So, I did not argue much. I was hungry at the time, so I spent the next hour at a bar nearby where I had a turkey bacon sandwich. Then, I caught the bus and came home somewhere around 7 p.m."

That is it. That was my perfect escape story to save myself. Now I only hoped for the cops to believe it.

"Was there anyone else in the garage with you, Nico?" He inquired.

"No, sir."

"And did you hear your uncle talk on the phone?"

"No, he always went out of the garage to talk."

I never knew I had it in me to lie so perfectly.

"Son, is there anything else you remember from yesterday?" He asked, pressingly.

"No," I nodded and said in an almost inaudible voice.

"Nico, if you remember anything, let us or your Papa know, okay?"

"Yes, sir!" I replied, finally looking up.

The cops took half of the day running back and forth, questioning each one of us. Then, they moved back to Papa, exchanged a few words, shook hands, and then left. There was a saddening and a deadly silence in the house. The ticking of the clock was the only loud sound you could hear in the quiet room.

No one knew what to say. Mama stood in the kitchen, preparing casseroles. Papa closed the door, walked toward the center of the room, and called on both Mama and me. All three of us sat on the dining table with our hands in front of us joined together. We remained silent, waiting for the other to speak up.

"There are going to be questions, a lot of them," said Papa. *"People will ask you what happened. The cops will ask you what happened,"* he said hinting toward both Mama and me. I had never seen my father look so sad and so broken. First, his son and now his brother. Was I to be blamed for all of this? Was I the cause of his grief? In a way, I blamed

myself because I think I could have prevented both of those deaths. If I wanted, I could have stood up and saved one of them, preventing this from happening. But I did not! I could have just told the truth to the police when the first murder occurred; when my uncle killed my brother in cold blood.

"I want you to know that the police will start their investigation, and we'll know who the murderer was. Till then, I want all of us to stick to each other. Marie, please call your parents and let them know. I'll call Mike's friends and let them know too. Till then, I'll be in the basement. Nico, you don't have to take Valerie to dance classes. Stay in your room, son, until we find out anything. Since it's a murder, the police won't give us the body. So, there's nothing we can do till then."

He got up from his chair and quietly walked toward the basement without saying another word.

"Mama," I broke the awkward silence. *"Can I go to my room?"* I asked to get excused.

"Yes, sure bambin," she said, maintaining her composure. I can tell she was trying to remain strong for her family.

***

I closed the door behind me, leaned against it, and broke down in tears. I could not control it anymore. The tears flowed like a never-ending night. My eyes burnt. My chest felt heavier carrying the lies, but now I felt like a weight had been lifted off it. I was a liar, I was a killer, and I was a coward – all those things I never wanted to be.

Finally, I was in my room where I could be myself and where I did not have to lie or pretend to be a good son. Was there any going back? If only I could turn back time to where we were as a family before – all of us together. All of a sudden, my mind wavered back to the dream I had on my last birthday. The one where I lost Carlo and was woken up by him. If only I could have done something then, but I was helpless.

My life was currently on the rocks, filled with lies, betrayal, murder, and conspiracy – all triggered by me. I am not sure why I blamed myself for all of this when I was only trying to make things better. But I guess I had no choice. I could not blame Mama and Papa for all that had happened. Uncle Mike was dead. I could not blame him either. Only I was left.

I somehow collected myself and threw myself on the bed. My clothes with bloodstains were still lying on the ground. I had to get rid of them. The clouds of regret and shame blurred my vision. My thoughts started to grow more and more entangled like a dark hole pulling me in its darkness that only became darker as I fell deeper into its pit.

"Nico, come down! We're waiting," yelled Carlo from down the hall.

"I'M COMING!" I screamed back.

"We're gonna start without you if you don't come soon," Carlo yelled again.

"I'm coming, I'm coming," I bellowed as I ran down the stairs into the family lounge.

"Hurry up bambin, we're just about to start the movie," Mama said as she saw me enter the room.

"I'm here, Mama," I said as I took my seat next to Valerie and Papa.

We were gonna watch *A Christmas Story*, which was basically a family tradition. Every Christmas Eve, we sat together as a family to watch old classics over Chinese food. It was something we voluntarily did as a kid, but as Carlo and I were getting older, we started to grow out of it. Carlo would go out with his friends on Christmas Eve, stay all night partying and drinking, and then come home early morning. But this year, Mama had put a good bargain, and we all had agreed to contribute to the traditional family night.

"What took you so long to come down, Nico?" Papa asked.

"He got lost staring outside his window and through Sophia's room, Papa," interrupted Carlo with a giggle.

"Shut up, Carlo, mind your business," I snapped.

"Boys, stop. The movie is about to start. Focus," Mama said.

I gave Carlo the ugliest look I could. He sneered from where he was sitting and mocked. The movie started. This was the first time Valerie was also a part of the tradition. She was excited more than any one of us.

We all watched the movie silently. It was a good day. We had bought presents for each other and Mama and Papa. I knew Carlo had a thing for action figures, so I had picked for him the latest collection of all the superheroes. It was a little pricey, but I had been saving money and wanted to give everyone the presents they wanted. I wanted it to be the best Christmas ever. We were halfway done with the movie when the doorbell rang twice. Irritated, I got up and went to open the door. It would probably be the delivery guy since we were expecting the Chinese food we had ordered for dinner.

"Coming," I yelled as I walked toward the door.

The bell continued ringing. It was loud and piercing through my ears.

"Urghhh…" I groaned as I opened the door.

A man was standing at the threshold. His clothes were stained with dried blood. His face was bruised and filled with blood too.

It was Uncle Mike standing at the door with the Chinese we ordered. I woke up panting again and dripping with sweat and a headache that had returned.

"Oh God, that was a dream, a bad, bad dream," I assured myself.

I lay there in bed for a few minutes, trying to gain back my consciousness. I did not realize that I had fallen asleep. The pillow was still wet from my crying. I wanted to get rid of the feelings of the regret and the guilt, and I was going to do anything to do that.

I got up from the bed as fast as I could and ran a cold shower in the bathroom. The water was cutting against my warm skin. I wish it could make my heart cold enough not to feel any emotions. I put on a new pair of pants and a clean flannel shirt and combed my hair neatly. I always combed my hair perfectly when it was a big day. And today was another big day for me.

Just like a hawk out for its prey, I headed downstairs to meet Papa. Today was the day I would make everything all right. I could not find him in the front room or the family lounge. I knew where he would be, so I drank a glass of water and made my way confidently to the basement. I had made up my mind. Nothing was going to stop me now.

I had to admit that I was nervous and scared. I hesitatingly knocked at the door and slightly opened the door. Papa was sitting on his desk with his reading glasses on. He was working on something but looked up when I knocked.

"Papa? Can I come in?" I asked.

My voice was almost shaking.

"Nico, come on in. Take a seat, son," Papa said.

The basement looked different than the last time I was there, or perhaps it was my mind playing games on me. Papa's desk was covered with files and papers. There was a cup of coffee that I remembered I had seen the last time too. The luminescent lights were brighter than ever. The chair opposite him was empty — the same place where I had found the gun that I shot Uncle Mike with.

"Wait ... the gun! Where did the gun go? I shot Uncle Mike, and I had the gun with me all that time."

I started recalling the events of the previous day to remember where exactly I lost the gun since it was not with me anymore.

"Where did I leave it? Did someone else find the gun? What if the police find out before anyone else?" I thought to myself as droplets of sweat started building up in my hands and on my forehead.

"Nico, are you okay?" Papa asked, bringing me back to reality.

"Yes ... yes ... yes, Papa," I mumbled.

"I said sit down, Nico" he repeated.

I took a seat in front of him. I could feel his stare on

me like he was aware of my dark secret. But how could he?

"How are you holding up, Nico?" Papa asked.

"I'm fine, Papa." I lied.

"Why are you sweating, son?" Papa asked.

"What? No ... nothing, Papa. I'm fine."

I panicked more, as I wiped the sweat from my forehead.

"So what do you want? How can I help you?" He asked.

I could not come up with a response or maybe a better lie, so I decided to stay quiet. I wondered what Papa was thinking at the moment. Did he realize his, son who was sitting across him was a murderer, liar, and manipulator? How long could I hide this from him and from everyone! I did not know how long I could hold up?

I sat there saying nothing. The strange thing was that Papa did not pester me to talk. We both sat there, waiting for the other to break the silence.

"Papa ..." I finally broke the tention after a few long minutes.

He looked up from his file again.

"Yes, Nico," he said.

"I ... I have something to tell you, Papa," I spoke with a shaking voice and body.

"Nico, I know, I already know," Papa said, looking straight at me.

Chapter 7
Uncertainty

"You know?" I asked confusingly.

"I know, Nico. And I've called off the police investigation. But I want to know why you did it. He was your Uncle, Nico."

"Papa ... I ... he killed Carlo, your son, and my brother." I screamed. *"I watched Uncle Mike kill Carlo, Papa."*

I screamed as tears flowed down my face.

"What are you talking about, Nico?" He looked sterner than before.

"I was there, Papa. It was me who watched him kill Carlo."

I showed persistence as I placed my fists on the desk. His face went white as if he had seen a ghost.

"Why didn't you tell me before, Nico?" He asked in a hoarse voice.

I continued crying and talking at the same time, *"I don't know Papa, I don't know."*

"You should have told me earlier, Nico. I could have sent Mike to prison. You did not have to kill him, dammit!" He was angry and loud.

"I'm sorry, I'm sorry," I continued to talk between the sobs.

"You think you can live with this, now? Live with being a murderer, a murderer of your own family?" He said, coming closer to me.

I could feel his warm breath on my face. I looked straight at him. His face was two inches away from mine. Too afraid to answer him, I simply shook my head in denial.

"What have you done, Nico? What have you done?" He repeated to himself, as he walked circling the room.

I sat there, shook to the core, salty tears dripping down my face into my mouth and on to Papa's desk, making a small pool. Nobody said a word for the next 10 minutes. After circling around in anger and distress, he came back to his desk and gulped a cup of coffee before taking his seat.

"Nico," he said.

I looked up with a runny nose and swollen eyes.

"I'm disappointed, son," he said with a straight face.

"I'm sorry, Papa," I said.

"I've already called off the investigation, Nico. But that does not mean I forgive you."

He took a short pause.

"I want you to become an integral part of the business. You're gonna leave school, Nico. And you will work full time and replace what you've done." He said.

"But ... Papa!" I looked up in shock. Was I hearing him right? *"I can't leave school."*

"No more buts. You will leave school, Nico. This is not a request, I'm not asking. This is what you will do. I want you in the business full-time."

"But, Papa, please," I was in tears again - this time even more intense. *"Please, Papa, I can't leave school. This is not a good business, Papa. We can do something else. Please understand. I don't want to do this,"* I begged.

"You should have thought of this before killing your uncle, Nico. It's decided. You're going to work from tomorrow on. I want you to take responsibility for this family and the business. I have to go to Virginia City to close a deal. Till then, I've asked someone to assist you from the

garage. They'll help you understand more of the business."

I continued sobbing with my head on the table.

"Go to your room, son."

I did not move.

"Nico," he shook me by the arm.

I looked up abruptly.

"Son, go to your room now. You start work tomorrow," he ordered.

***

"How long will you be visiting, Marcus?" Mama asked Papa, sitting on her side of the bed.

"Don't worry, Marie. I'll be back in a few days. You take care of the house and the kids until then," he said as he packed his suitcase.

"I'm scared, Marcus. The house will be so empty, so quiet. What if ..."

"Nothing will happen, Marie. Nico is in the house. He'll take care of things," Papa said.

"He's still a kid, Marcus. Why don't you tell me why he has to leave school?"

She stood up from the bed and came close to him, standing next to him and looking straight at him. She was on the verge of crying.

"Just trust me, Marie. I'm doing what's good for everyone, okay?" He said, putting his hands on her shoulders in an assuring way.

She took a breath of relief and sat down on the bed.

"And what about you, Marcus? How do I know you'll be fine?" She asked.

"Marie, you need to relax. This is not the first time I'm going on a business trip. I'll be fine, my love." He assured her again, this time looking into her eyes.

"Marcus, can I ask you something?" She said.

"Yeah ... sure," he replied.

"I think there's something wrong with Nico."

Papa's eyebrows furrowed.

"What do you mean, Marie?"

"I think he's upset. I think he's hiding something from us. I can see it in his eyes, Marcus," she said, gripping his arm tightly.

"Marie, my angel, don't overthink this. Nico is fine. I've spoken with him many times. He's lost his brother and uncle in a very short period of time. Of course, he's upset. But there's nothing he's hiding. Try to stop thinking about it."

Meanwhile, I had locked myself in the room and cried with Chloe by my side. Nothing was going to make me feel better, not even her soft fur skin, her pout face, or her wet kisses. I felt trapped inside my own house, my own room, my own mind, and there was no escaping.

If only I had thought this through. Perhaps this was my punishment for not saving Carlo. No one could save me from this mess that I had created. I was being pulled in the same life my father had lived. But this was not something I had asked for, so why me?

"I guess I am left with no option. Maybe this is the life I am supposed to live. If I give in, things will start making sense." I thought to myself.

But not today! Today, I was not ready for that life. I ducked under my bed for the steel box I had hidden, filled with action figures and weed that Luca had given me. Today, this was my only escape. It took me a few minutes to recall the way Luca had taught me to roll a joint. I was careful and successful. I took a long puff of smoke, infiltrating my lungs with its toxicity. It felt good and relieving. I took another puff, this one stronger than the first one. I could feel the heaviness both in my chest and head. It felt dizzy but good. I was in a new world, slightly better than the one I was already living in. I swirled and danced. I was smiling – my eyes shiny and glassy.

A feeling of ecstasy mixed with the warm blood in my veins circulated in every part of my body. I was up in the clouds with Carlo. I could see his face closer to mine. He was in a happy place. I could see myself going near him as I closed my eyes and surrender into the overwhelming euphoria.

***

The next morning, I woke up with a recurring headache and the sweet smell of fried bacon. I had not eaten anything since the previous afternoon. My stomach was growling from fear and hunger. Without wasting much time, I ran downstairs to meet Papa before he left for Virginia City. I searched his room, the basement, and the front lounge. He was nowhere to be found. Mama was in the kitchen, as always, making breakfast.

"Nico, bambin, sit down, and have breakfast. Your Papa told me you'd be taking care of the business from today."

I sat on the chair, grabbing a slice of fried bacon from the plate.

"Mama, where's Papa?" I asked, looking sideways.

"Honey, he already left. He has left you that package."

She pointed out to a Manila envelope lying across the table. I quickly moved forward to grab the envelope. There was nothing in it except a few hundred dollars and papers with numbers and names on it.

"Nico, have your breakfast first. You have all day for this, son."

I sat back on my chair and looked at my mother.

"Mama," I said

"Yes, Nico," she said as she fumbled with the dishes on the table.

"You said you would help me. You said you wouldn't let me be a part of the business. What happened, Mama? Why didn't you help me?"

I did not mean to accuse my mother. I was just looking for answers, but the hurt in her eyes was so apparent. I had messed up again. Of all people, I did not want to hurt my mother. I wished I could take my words back the instant I let them out of my mouth.

"I'm sorry, Nico." This was all she said and then walked back to the kitchen, hiding her tears.

I ate the rest of my breakfast in silence. After I was done, I quietly walked out of the house and toward the bus stop to go to the garage. The rest of the day went by pretty fast. I watched the men do their jobs and asked them a few questions. Rodrigo and Santiago showed me around and taught me how to know if the shipment was correct. It was hard to understand all the jargons and terms they used.

It would take me days to understand them. I tried hard to keep my head into what I was being taught, but I could not stop thinking about school. Today was the first day after summer. I could not stop thinking about Luca and Marie Ann either. I felt left out. I had not told Luca anything, but I was sure he would come around soon, wondering something was not right. Till then, I had to try to keep my mind away from things I could not get.

The garage got closed at 6 p.m. It was not a tiring day but definitely a boring one. I could not wait to go home, lie on my bed, and play with Chloe. I reached home a little after 7:30 p.m. Mama and Valeri were watching cartoons together. I simply wanted to go to bed, so I tried to walk without making any sound.

"Hey, Nico" shouted Mama from across the room.

I turned back in disappointment.

"Umm... yes, Mama."

"Son, come here and join us. We'll watch TV together. I'll get you dinner, too," she said enthusiastically.

"Mama. I'm not so hungry and I ... I was thinking to go to bed directly. If Papa calls, let him know the day went fine."

Her face fell.

"Oh okay, son, it's okay, I understand. You sleep well," she said with a smile.

***

"Stephen, I'm on my way, just hold on," said Papa, who was driving west of Virginia City to close an important deal.

"Look, Marcus if you don't get here in the next 15 minutes, I'll cancel all the shipments," said Stephen on the other side of the line.

"I'll be there. Just wait for me," said Papa with anger.

This was supposed to be a lifetime deal. Stephen and Papa had been together in the business for a long time. They had grown up together. When Papa moved to America, Stephen was the first friend he made. They both had started the business together; but after getting married, Papa had moved to San Francisco and started everything from scratch. Stephen was mad in the beginning, but years later, their friendship rekindled, and they became partners again.

"I'm almost there, Stephen," said Papa.

He shut the phone and drove faster than before. It was 9 p.m., and the roads were already empty. It was a small town, and not many people roamed the streets aimlessly at night. Papa was unfamiliar with most of the streets, but this one, he had traveled a lot in his early days. It took 10 more minutes to reach an empty warehouse that was located behind a small pub. It was a Tuesday night, and the pub was not so crowded. He hoped to get a drink to quench his thirst, but he did not want Stephen to wait any longer, so he thought he would grab the drink later with his old friend over a good conversation. He quickly made a sharp turn along the right corner of the street and stopped at a warehouse that said, *"Steph & Company."* He saw the signboard and chuckled under his breath.

"Stephen always loved the spotlight," he thought to himself.

He waited for a few minutes before knocking. He took a deep breath, straightened his pants, and stretched a little. His back hurt from driving for six long hours. He took another deep breath and knocked harder on the door.

"Stephen, it's me, Marcus!"

He waited for a few more minutes when a tall, dark, bald man opened the door.

"Evening," Papa said. *"I'm looking for Stephen. I'm Marcus."* He extended his hand.

The tall man did not shake his hand and simply moved aside to give Papa some way inside. Papa entered a huge warehouse. It was perfectly lit and packed with cardboard boxes, with not much place to walk. It was congested and difficult to breathe inside. He loosened the top two buttons of his shirt to let some air inside.

The man led him deeper inside of the warehouse. It was a long, endless walk that finally ended next to an old rusty desk, a few chairs, and big lamps. Five men were sitting around the desk. One of them was Stephen.

"Stephen!" Papa said with excitement. *"My man, how are you doing?"* He hugged him and patted his back.

"You're late, Marcus."

One could judge that Stephen meant strictly business since he did not greet Papa in return.

"I've been driving for six hours," said Papa taking a seat opposite Stephen.

"Did you bring the money?" Asked Stephen.

"So, no hello! No, how are you?" Papa asked.

"I don't have time for that, Marcus," said Stephen.

Stephen was almost 5'7" with blonde hair and green eyes. His birthmark was prominent on his left arm – a dark black rough patch. His lips naturally formed an arch when he spoke. His voice sounded hoarse. Even though the inside of the warehouse was burning with heat, he wore jeans, a shirt, and a leather jacket. He was always good at math. When Papa and Stephen worked together, Stephen always looked after the money while Papa dealt with the clients. But today it felt like Papa was meeting a different Stephen. He felt like his old friend had changed a lot over time.

"Where is the money, Marcus?" He asked again.

Papa rubbed his eyes.

"I'm a bit short, Stephen. I need some more time."

"I can't give you more time, Marcus," Stephen said.

"My son died a few months back and now my brother," Papa explained.

"Yeah, and if you don't give me my money, you will be next," he said with a smirk.

"What's gotten into you, Steph? Why are you acting this way?"

The other four men in the room stood their ground, waiting patiently for orders from Stephen. They had rifles in their hands. They looked like men from action movies – broad shoulders, tall height, muscular arms, and well-groomed mustaches. These are the kind of men you never want to mess with. All they needed was a reason to kill you and bury your body without letting a soul know.

"Dammit! Marcus! Cut the crap. You told me you were gonna get the money. Are a hundred envelopes not enough for me to remind you? You've been ignoring my calls, not responding to my emails, how do I know you're not gonna run away, huh?" Said a heated Stephen with his hands on the desk and his face red with anger. *"This was your last fuckin' chance!"*

"Calm down Steph, just give me two months. I'll get it all figured out," Said Papa calmly.

Stephen walked back and forth with a gun in his hand and his face red with rage. He continuously revolved the gun around his fingers.

"No ... no, it's too late," he pulled out a joint from his pocket, lit it, and took a long puff, inhaling internally.

"What's the matter, Stephen? Why are you panicking? You don't you trust me?" Papa asked.

"Trust you?" His laugh echoed in the warehouse. *"You abandoned me, Marcus. You left me here and moved to San Francisco. I was on my own. I had to start all this on my own."*

"I tried to contact you, Steph, but you didn't answer my calls. I was starting a family. I had to make decisions."

"Yeah... Well, fuck you and your family," Stephen bellowed.

"Easy, Stephen. You're acting crazy now," Papa said with anger running through his veins.

They both were standing face to face, looking straight into each other's eyes.

"Look Stephen, everything will be fine, just like the old days," Papa said.

"Nothing can be the same, Marcus. It's been too long. All I want is the money you owe me," he said as he pulled the gun's hammer back and pointed it at Papa's head.

"What are you doing, Stephen? I'm your friend," explained Papa.

"You're not. No one is my friend. Friends make you weak!" Before Stephen could say anything else, Papa tried to pull the gun out of his hands.

They both held tightly to its body, going back and forth, pointing the nozzle at each other in turns. It was a tough fight. None of them was going to give up that easily. It continued for the next few minutes and stopped when one of the men from the back hit Papa behind the head with the stock of the gun. It was a loud thud. Papa held his head in his hand as he fell to the ground. He growled in pain. Stephen took his turn next and kicked Papa in the gut. He lay there, helpless, knocked out from the blow of the gun.

"C'mon boys," Stephen motioned his men to follow him out of the warehouse.

While Papa lay inside of the warehouse, Stephen closed the warehouse door from the outside. He wanted to make sure that Papa did not escape. He then ordered his men to burn the warehouse down.

Inside, Papa gained consciousness. He got up struggling and holding on to his head that hurt from the blow. Limping and struggling, he made his way to the main door. It was closed. He tried hard to open the door, but it was heavy and closed from the outside. There was a small window from which he could look outside into the street.

On the outside, Stephen and his men threw gasoline on the walls of the warehouse. They covered the entire warehouse with fuel. The smell was pungent and reached Papa's nostrils too. He tried breaking the window but found no luck. One of the men took out a silver Zippo lighter from his pocket, lit the lighter by snapping his fingers, and tossed it toward the warehouse form a distance. The entire building glowed in bright yellow flames. The flames grew higher and higher. The inside of the warehouse grew hotter. Papa continued to struggle and fight for life on the inside. His breathing became heavier and fainter with every passing minute. The flames reached the inside of the warehouse. The empty cardboard boxes, wooden desks, and everything else caught fire immediately. Papa took off his shirt to fight the growing heat inside of the warehouse.

He looked around and found a heavy stone nearby. He tried breaking the window with the stone. After several tries, he succeeded, but there was not much he could do with the increasing fire on the inside. He was running short of breath, his breathing palpating. He looked outside of the window gasping for air, but his pants were already on fire. There was not much he could do now.

He was running out of breath and life. Papa kneeled on the ground and leaned back on the door. Sweat dripping from his face, marked with bruises and dark spots. All he could think about was his family; Carlo, Nico, and Valerie. His three kids and wife occupied his mind in his last moments. He had promised Marie he would be fine, but little did he know that he was unaware of his fate. Memories of them together eating meals, watching movies as a family kept playing and fading simultaneously. He tried to hold on to them longer. The memories of Valerie's birth, Nico's first steps, and Carlo's first trophy were the only soothing thoughts in that moment of fight and fury. With every second, it became a blur. His eyes felt heavier. His breathing almost completely gone, as he was trying to complete one last prayer, he gasped *'Hail Mary, Full of Grace. The Lord is with Thee.'* There was no more left in him as he closed his eyes and let go.

***

It was 2 a.m. in San Francisco. I had slept early when I came home from the garage and woke up an hour ago to go downstairs and grab something to eat. I fetched myself some cold chicken pieces, cranberry sauce, and coleslaw. I made myself a good sandwich and came back to my room to smoke a joint and eat in peace.

Mama and Valerie were sound asleep in their room. The days when Papa was away, both of them slept in the same room. I sat at my window, looking at the dark blue sky with constellations tracing the clouds. The sky was clear, and the night was chilly. It was a lot peaceful than it usually is in the day. I could hear the distant sound of a phone ringing. It rang twice and thrice. Annoyed, I got out of my room and was halfway downstairs when I saw Mama answering the phone.

"Who in the right mind would call at this time?" I thought to myself.

I stood there impatiently, while Mama spoke on the phone.

"Marcus," she screamed on top of her lungs and fell to the ground sobbing.

I ran downstairs as fast as I could and pulled Mama in my arms.

"Mama, what happened? Mama?" I asked panicking.

She continued crying without saying a word.

"Mama, tell me what happened. Who was on the phone?" I asked again.

"Nico, your father is dead," she cried.

"What?" I yelled.

I felt my body growing lifeless. Somebody had sucked the life out of me. I rubbed my eyes to see if this was just another scary dream, but it was not. Mama and I lay there on the cold floor, holding on to each other in the middle of the night. Bad luck had struck our family once again. This was probably the longest night of my life.

Chapter 8
Plan to Escape

It had been two weeks since the sad demise of my father hit my family like a hurricane. Families from different parts of the city were coming over to visit us and offer their condolences. Many wanted to pay their respects. People who knew Papa crowded our house – his friends, workers, and my grandparents – everyone who knew and cared for him. Grandma even offered to stay for a while, but Mama was determined that she would take care of her family all by herself.

At nights when I passed by her room, I could hear her cry and sob, yet there was nothing I could say or do to comfort her or ease her pain. The next morning, she would wake up as if nothing had happened. She would keep a straight face, trying to convince the world that she was taking it fine; that she was strong enough to forget first her son's and then her husband's death.

"If only I had her strength," I thought to myself.

We had not sat as a family since the tragedy occurred. There was not much left of the family, but whatever little was left was broken from the inside. Nobody knew how Papa died. The police said that someone had left a burning cigarette in the warehouse, which probably caused the fire. My father's case was dead just like him, and the murderers roamed the city like free birds. My nightmares started to become worse too. Most of the nights, I stayed up late, thinking, crying, and hoping if it was me instead of Papa. What were we gonna do without him? How were we gonna do anything without him? I was just 15 years old.

How was I supposed to take the responsibility of the entire house? Where was the money gonna come from? With Papa's death, does it mean that I don't have to be a part of the business? My mind boggled with unanswered questions – all of them overlapping with each other, entangling in a web that I was unable to escape.

I sat on the windowsill with my knees against my chest, looking at the clear sky, and trying to find a star that resembled Papa and Carlo. They were both united now, watching above us and protecting us, or was it just in my mind? Sometimes, I would think of running away, but where would I go? What about Mama and Valerie? The thoughts of leaving my family dug a deeper hole in my chest, but I was not ready for this challenge.

"Knock ... knock," there was a loud thud on my room's door, as I sat against the window on one of the nights.

"Come in," I yelled.

The door opened slightly. Mama, dressed in her nightgown, walked into my room.

"Nico," she said in her soft voice.

"Mama, is everything okay?" I asked as I walked toward her and placed my hand under her arm.

"Yes, yes, everything is fine, son. Sit down, please," She sat on the edge of my bed. *"Nico, I just came to talk to you.*

"Yes ... yes sure, Mama. What is it?"

I took place next to her.

"How are you holding up, bambin?" She asked.

"I'm okay, Mama. I'll be fine," I lowered my eyes.

"Son, this year has been hard for us. All of us. I'm sorry for what you had to go through. I can't bring your father or brother back, but I can promise to be your rock. I promise to be there for you and Valerie. But..."

She took a small pause.

"But," she started again. *"I want you to continue working*

for your Papa's business, Nico." Tears fell down her eyes. *"I know you hate it. I know you don't want to be a part of it. But, Nico, you already know about the business. You know that we need money. And this business is the only memory of your father that we have. Son, I want you to continue working for it."*

As soon as she was done talking, her face fell, and she lowered her eyes. Her warm tears fell on my hand.

"Do you really want me to do this, Mama?" I asked with a shaky voice.

She nodded hastily. We both sat on the bed, holding each other's hands and not saying a single word.

"Okay, Mama," was all I could mutter, not knowing if I really meant it or not.

"Thank you, Nico. Thank you for that, my child," she said through the tears.

She held my head in her hands and kissed my forehead with her wet lips. How could I say no to my mother in despair? But how could I lie to myself either? In the struggle between my head and my heart, I was the one who was losing. I was losing control over myself.

I have not been in touch with Luca. I had seen him last at Papa's funeral. He and Marie Ann had come together. I was a little jealous, but there were other more important things on my mind than to cry over a girl. So basically, I had no friends, no one to confide in, and no one to share my thoughts with. After Mama left the room, I just lay flat on my bed, staring at the walls and contemplating. I was expected to be the leader of the house.

I was expected to pay the bills and bring money. So many unrealistic expectations put on me, only pushed me further down. Since Papa's death, I had been spending most of my time in my room, so did Mama. My room was the place where I had been doing most of the thinking and crying. The rest of the house seemed so haunted, so vacant with two of the family members missing.

"Missing..." I thought.

"What If I go missing? What if I flee and never return? Would that liberate me from all expectations and responsibilities?" I thought.

A new ray of hope shone brightly through me. I immediately got up from the bed, grabbed my laptop, and started looking for a place I could run to, where I could safely hide. Should I make a planned escape or a surprise one? Either way, it was decided that I was running away. I spent the rest of the day, planning and packing. I emptied my old backpack and filled it with some clothes, toothbrush, toothpaste, comb, some weed, and snacks that I had sneaked from the kitchen. I planned to sneak some more snacks and steal some money from Mama's wallet at night when she was asleep.

I could not go to Luca's place, as Mama would know where I was. After some researching and thinking, I decided to crash at Papa's warehouse for some time. My escape plan already sounded a success to me. I only had to wait for the night to take over now.

Throughout lunch, I was restless and ate too fast. Mama noticed.

"Nico, what's the hurry? Are you alright?" She asked.

"Yes, yes, Mama, I'm fine," I said, avoiding all eye contact.

I wanted to get out of the room as soon as possible and finish my packing for the escape. I did not want this to be another one of my stupid decisions, so I planned carefully and thought it through a few hundred times. It was going to be now or never. Around 9 p.m., Mama put Valeri to bed. She went to the kitchen, made herself some tea, walked back to her room, and closed the door. I took the opportunity and grabbed some cold sausages, a bottle of jam, a loaf of bread, and some chips to take along. I quickly walked to my bedroom and threw all of it in my backpack. Only one last thing was left to do. I had to wait for Mama to fall asleep, then take some money from her bag.

I waited outside of her room for her lights to go off. The clock on the corridor walls struck 9:45 p.m. The wait was getting longer, and I was growing impatient too. The bus for the other part of the town would be taking off at 10:10 p.m. I had to reach the bus stop before that or else my plan would fail. Five minutes later, the lights in Mama's room went off. My breathing grew heavier.

I knew I had to be extremely careful and try not to make a sound. I waited for another five minutes before entering her room. It was too dark for me to see anything. I followed the trail of light coming from under the door. Mama kept her bag in her closet. The money was in her bag that I needed to get my hands on. I took small steps and opened the door of her closet, hoping it did not make the screeching sound it usually did. I wanted to be fast, so I opened the door carefully as I looked behind at Mama sleeping soundly and unaware of me sneaking in her room. Her red colored bag lay on the first shelf. I quietly leaned against the closet door and took out five, one hundred dollar bills. I did not know how long I would be able to live with that money, but at that point, I could use every single penny that I found. I put the bag back where it was and closed the closet door, trying not to wake Mama up.

As soon as I stepped out of her room, I sighed a breath of relief. It was better to hurry before she woke up and found me lurking in the hallways. I ran to my room and packed my bag with the remaining clothes. Before leaving, I cleaned my bedroom and changed the sheets. I took a good, long look outside the window. The lights in Sophie's room were switched off. It did not surprise me.

I stepped out of the room, closed the door behind me, and quietly made my way downstairs and out of the house. I did not look behind because I knew it would only make it challenging for me to keep moving. I did not want the emotional ties and memories to pull me back from running away. The streets were quiet, and there was not a soul to be found anywhere. I walked toward the bus stop. Several cars passed by me, honking, probably wondering what a 15-year-old boy was doing at this time of the night. I remained focused and continued to walk toward my destination. The bus stop was empty too, except in a distance where a homeless man lay with a cloth over his head, snoring the night away. I stood there impatiently, waiting for the bus to come. I kept looking at my wristwatch. The time on the watch struck 10:10. The bus should be here any minute.

A few minutes passed when a bus came and stopped in front of me. I ran inside and sat on the third seat from the left. The driver looked at me in confusion, probably thinking why an adult did not accompany me. I avoided his gaze and started looking outside the window. Apart from me, there were four more people on the bus, perhaps going to the same place I was or maybe somewhere else.

It took us faster than usual to reach the remote town in the distant. Since the bus stopped at a further distance, I had to walk for 20 more minutes to reach the garage. I was scared to walk alone at this hour of the day. The houses in this part of the town were strangely quiet, and the streets were dark too. I could distinctly hear a dog barking in the distance somewhere. It grew fainter as I continued to walk. One of the houses had lights switched on, and I could hear a man and a woman fighting.

The man sounded drunk, and the woman was crying loudly. I put the voices behind me and walked as fast as I could. I reached the garage and dug into my backpack pockets for the keys to the shutter. It was big and bulky. I had never opened a shutter myself before. I struggled hard, but I was not going to give up this easily. I used all my force and pushed the shutter up with all my strength. I failed once, twice, but the third time, I succeeded. I pushed the shutter with one hand and forced myself inside the garage with the other.

The inside on the garage was dark and hot. I knew where the light switches were. The first thing I did was to turn them on. The people of this town knew Papa very well. He was their only source of income. I could not afford them knowing that his son was secretly hiding in his garage, so I shut the shutter door behind and only turned on one light to help me get by. I am lucky that I was able to find one clean spot in the garage where I decided to put the sheet that I had stolen from the home. I made myself comfortable and decided to get familiar with my new home.

***

"Nico, honey come down. Breakfast is ready. You have to go to Papa's garage," yelled Mama, from the kitchen.

No reply. She had been calling out for me for half an hour, but there was no reply.

"Valerie, sweetheart, can you please go and wake your brother up?" Mama said.

"Yes, Mama," said an excited Valerie.

She ran upstairs in her pink shorts and a white t-shirt that read, *'Mommy's Little Princess.'* She struggled to reach the doorknob but was able to open the door with some grit and hard work.

"Nico, wake up," she said in her baby voice as she entered the room.

There was no one in the room. The bed was empty and perfectly made. Little Valerie walked back downstairs and informed Mama.

"What do you mean he's not in the room, Valerie?" Mama said annoyingly.

She put the TV on to distract Valerie and walked to my room to check herself.

"Nico, you're making me come upstairs, you should

better be up and dressed son," said Mama breathlessly.

She entered the room to find no one was there. The room was strangely clean. She knocked on the bathroom door to check if I was inside.

"Nico, you there?" She screamed.

No reply either! She opened the bathroom door abruptly and found no one inside.

"Where did this boy go?" She thought to herself.

Maybe he left early for the garage that would explain the missing sausages. She closed the door behind and went back downstairs. My absence went almost unnoticed for the rest of the day.

Around 7 p.m., Mama started to wonder where I was. The garage did not have a phone, and she had nowhere to call to ask my whereabouts. She sat on the dining table to keep her mind occupied and away from me. She busied herself with Valerie.

They both made each other play, watched cartoons, and danced around to music. Eventually, Valerie grew tired and wanted to go to bed. Mama read her a book and sang her a lullaby. Time was passing so fast. It was at 9 p.m. when she began to panic. She searched for Luca's number and phoned him.

"Hello, is this Luca, Nico's friend?" She said on the phone.

"Hello, yes I am, who's this?" He asked.

"Luca, honey. I'm Marie. Nico's mother."

"Marie, is everything okay?" He asked, concerned.

"Luca, do you know where Nico is? I haven't seen him the whole day, and I don't know where he could be? Do you have any idea where he would be?" She asked.

"I'm sorry, Marie. I have no idea where Nico would be. I haven't seen him since Marcus' funeral."

He was not lying.

"Luca, if you hear anything from him, please call me, sweetheart," she said.

"Sure, Marie, I'll let you know. Have a nice evening." he then hung up.

***

Two days passed since I had run away from home. Mama had been devastated. She searched the entire neighborhood and called all my classmates and my street friends, yet found no clue of where I was. She would send Valerie to the neighbor's house and spend all her day crying and looking for me. I lay in the garage, covered in dirt and a stinking smell of rats. Every morning, I hid my sheets and bag, so the workers could not figure out that I had run away from home. The food was about to spoil, and I was sick of eating cold sausages.

I could use the money, but I did not know when I would need it, so I kept the bills safe under the pile of clothes in my bag. I will be lying if I say I did not miss the comfort of my home and cold water running down my body, washing away all my thoughts and bruises. But most of all, I missed Mama and Valerie. I missed the warm food in front of me that Mama placed every morning – my favorite blueberry pancakes and fried bacon.

I missed Valerie's singing and dancing in the hallways that was the first thing you would hear if you wake up in my house. In short, I missed the life I left behind. My clothes were dirty, and I had not showered in days now. Soon the workers could smell betrayal and disgust with me. But I had nowhere else to go, no one else to ask for help. The only choice I had was to accept my fate, go back, and continue with life as if nothing ever happened. Maybe this was what would make Mama happy, Valerie happy, and me happy. If it would make my family happy, then this was what I should be doing, instead of being selfish and running away like a coward. My thoughts were contradicting my beliefs. The same was with my head and heart. They were fighting against each other. I am not sure what I was thinking, but just like all the plans and ideas I made in the past and failed, this was going to fail too. Perhaps, I had no choice but to accept life, walk in the footsteps of my father, and continue his legacy. I packed my things immediately and ran to the nearest bus stop to catch a bus back home. I could not wait to go home, hug Mama, and eat the food she had made.

I could not wait to play with my little sister and take her back to dancing classes. On my way back home, I realized that we could be a family again, we could live happily, even if that meant I would have to give up on my dreams. If that is what brings my family together, then so be it. If that is what makes Papa and Carlo happy, then that is precisely what I will do. On my way back home, I promised myself never to abandon my family again. Perhaps that was what Papa had been trying to tell me all along. And I only understood it after his death. Family sticks together.

Chapter 9
No Longer a Choice

Things started to go back to normal. Of course, without Papa and Carlo, we could never be normal again, but the smile on Mama's face was returning. Valerie was growing into a beautiful young girl. What once felt like an amateur dancing routine was now turning into professional dancing. Two years passed since the worst time of my family had ended. We could never forget that year, no matter how much we tried. It stayed in our minds always like a bad memory.

I finally accepted my fate and started working at the garage every day since the day I returned home and confessed to Mama. I took over Papa's office in the basement, did some renovation, and made it a little modern as per my preference. We now spent more time as a family. We ate dinner together every night and spoke about how our days went. Some nights we went out to eat. I could tell how happy it made my Mama to see all three of us together in one room, sharing laughter and memories together. She was aging. Her eyes were filled with sadness, but her face was filled with hope.

She talked about finding me a girl and playing with my children, but I always waived the thought off, by saying I was too young to even think of marriage. I had completely surrendered myself to the business. The workers in the garage liked me, just as much as they liked Papa. They were happy to see me there every day. It took me some time in the beginning, but I eventually understood the nitty-gritty of it. I actually started to like the garage. Most of the workers spoke Italian. Sometimes when there was not enough work, we would just sit, talk, and drink beers. I had been spending so much time in that part of the town that the locals started to recognize me and invite me to their houses. I also offered jobs to the men of the town, just as my father did.

Last year in summer, when the monsoon season was on its peak, the streets were flooded with rainwater, the rain continued to fall for two straight weeks, and going back to home and coming back to the garage was not possible, I was invited by a local house in the town where I ate and slept. There lived a woman with her husband and their daughter, who was about my age. I sat there in their kitchen, waiting for food when she first walked in. She was a pleasing sight to see. I have to admit, the moment I laid my eyes on her, I forgot all about Sophia and Marie Ann. Her soft blue eyes, petite body, and long blonde hair had me falling for her from the minute she walked in the kitchen. I was too shy to talk, so I continued to catch glimpses for her for the number of days I stayed at their house. One fine day, when her parents had to leave the house to go somewhere, I grew the courage to speak to her. Her name was Molly Amelia. She looked at me with her soft blue eyes and told me all about her life. Without realizing the time, we spoke for three long hours. I could feel the connection growing with every passing second. It was strange yet special. It felt like I had known her all my life.

I soon confessed my love for Molly Amelia, a month later to her family. They were elated to hear that the man they admired so much was in love with their only daughter. I took Molly Amelia on our first date. We ate crab cakes, drank champagne, and spoke about the future, our future. After dinner, I had the urge to hold her in my arms and caress her face. I hesitated a little and then grabbed her hands and slowly kissed her lips gently with mine. She smelled like a rose dipped in honey, and her lips tasted like bubble gum from her pink lip-gloss. At that moment, I knew she was the one I wanted to marry and spend the rest of my life with. But it was too early.

I wanted to continue working for Papa's business and expand it to other cities. I wanted to stand on my own feet before I asked her hand in marriage. So, we continued dating and meeting each other. I was always welcomed by her family. They showed their greatest affection and showered all their love on me.

It's true that time passes fast when you are too busy making the most of it. Meeting Molly Amelia changed me for the better, in every way. It gave me hope. I wanted to work harder than ever to provide for my family. Even though things were going fine, I felt like Luca and I drifted apart without saying much to each other. I blame most of it on myself. I was jealous and did not want to let anyone in at that time, but it was time now for me to rekindle my friendship with him.

It had been two years since we last spoke or saw each other. Two weeks back, I finally pushed myself to show up at his house. It was awkward and uncomfortable at first, but we both fought a little, cried a little, and then hugged each other like brothers. I came clean to Luca about my past and what had really happened. It came to him as a shock more than it did to me. He was still dating Marie Ann. After finishing high school, she had flown to New York to get a master's degree, but he stayed back to attend community college and work in the city. I was happy that he was happy. Before leaving, I made sure to return the 500 dollars I had borrowed from him two years ago. He was surprised that I remembered. We both shared a laugh together and promised to stay in touch.

That reminds me that I will be receiving an important shipment today, and it was vital for me to be present in the garage. I shut the thoughts off, took a cold shower, and ran downstairs to catch breakfast. There was no sight of Mama in the kitchen. Lately, she had been waking up earlier than me. She would prepare breakfast for both Valerie and me and go back to her room. A plate of scrambled eggs and toasted bread lay on the table for me. I grabbed a few small bites and left the house without saying goodbye.

That was the routine. She would know that I had left for work from my half-eaten eggs. It assured her that I was not running away again. It was a nice sunny day. The sun shone brightly in the sky, and the roads were clear too. I had stopped taking the bus until last year when I received my driving license and drove to work every day. The workers had already started piling boxes, making calls, and receiving shipments for the day. I said my usual hello and made a track of the entire month's accounts. The day went normally until midday when a young worker brought me two letters. One was signed by *Mr. Katz*, and the other had no name. It was strange that after so many years, Mr. Katz had sent me a letter. I tore open the sealing and began reading the letter signed by him first. It read,

Dear Nico,

It's been years since we last met, hope you are doing well.

Nico, I am extremely sorry for the loss your family has borne in the last few years. I cannot imagine the pain you and your family have gone through, please accept my condolences. I'll always remember you in my prayers, son.

Son, I hope you read this letter first. I understand that you must be confused, seeing two letters. The anonymous letter is from your father, Nico. He left that letter to me, to give it to you when you were of age.

Your father was a good man, Nico. He was kind and compassionate. He was a great father, a loving husband, and a supportive friend. I hope you remember him in the kindest words. I had promised him to keep the letter safe, and only give it to you when you're ready. I have heard that you have taken over the business and are doing well. This is why I think it's time you read your father's last words that he left you with.

Hope to see you soon,

Miriam Katz

Another letter Papa had left for me. I immediately opened the second later and recognized his slanted writing style. It was definitely by Papa and read,

My beloved Nico,

By the time you'll receive this letter, I'll be long gone. I hope this letter finds you in good health. I'm sure after I'm gone, you'll be a good boy to your mother and an amazing brother to your sister. Take care of them, my child.

I'm sure you have taken over the business just as I wanted you to. You've always made me proud, Nico. I know you'll continue to do the same. Son, forgive me for choosing your life for you, but trust me, Nico, I'm looking out for you like I always have. After I'm gone, I want you to take over both the business and the house. Take care of your family, for the family is what you live for.

Make sure your sister receives a good education and look out for her, Nico. Respect your mother, and tell her how much I loved her. Make sure there's never a tear in her eyes. She deserves all the happiness in the world, son. Most of all, Nico, I want you to know that you are a strong and brave man. You are probably not the 15-year-old kid anymore. You must have been a grown man when this letter reaches you.

I believe in you, Nico, and I believe that you will look out for your family and make the right decisions. You are so much stronger than I could ever imagine you'd be. I love you, my son.

Yours truly,

Papa

I sat there in silence for the next five minutes, unable to move or say a word. Papa knew he was going to die. He knew I would be left to take on his legacy, yet he never said a word about it. He remained calm till his last breath. But why did he not fight for his life, why did he not fight to live, why did he accept it as his fate? These are questions that I will never have the answers to. The questions that will haunt me for the rest of my life. He died with my secret inside him. He never told a soul about it. I failed to understand him, the person he was. When everyone in this town and even his friends loved him, appreciated him, and celebrated his name, I was the only one hating him for choosing this life for me.

Did I fail as a son to Papa? I would never know. But I can try to be the son he wanted. I can try to be the man he wished to see in me. I can be the same that everyone loves, and who is appreciated and cherished. I can be kind to my workers and be there for my family in their good and bad times. I hope Papa can see the man I have become, and how far I have come. Even though I have made terrible decisions and regretted most of them, yet I can try to become the best version of myself that he always wanted me to be.

A smile spread across my face. A part of me knew Papa was there looking out for me, protecting me, and guiding me. That explains the reason I have come so far. It describes how far I have come. Today, in my heart, there is nothing except love for my father and my family. You see, I was made to believe since childhood that family is all you have till the very end.

You live for your family, and you die for your family. My father died for his family, and I will live as he wanted me to, for my family. I was made to believe that I was meant to be a gangster. I never wanted to be a gangster. Now I know, I never really had a choice.

www.ingramcontent.com/pod-product-compliance
Lightning Source LLC
Chambersburg PA
CBHW022158240626
47153CB00007B/2718